"Tell you what, sweetheart, the on'- taking any notice of the next few ... cal one that lets me ᴸ- eat...(

"And everything else, Look, is that a pub ahead?"

"Gerald seems to think so ... ... out into a...a fast walk, I suppose you

Phil's less than complime... ...escription of Gerald's speed was a little bit unfair, but if truth were to be told, not by very much. Gerald was definitely getting long in the tooth, but good for a few more years of tourism before a well-earned retirement field beckoned.

The hand-crafted sign outside the pub stated without fuss the patently obvious fact that this was indeed Michael Ashe's Pub, their first night's scheduled stop. Even before they drew onto the forecourt, a young lad of at least thirteen or fourteen appeared from somewhere behind the pub, wearing a leather apron and carrying a metal pail.

The pail hit the ground immediately in front of Gerald's eager muzzle; a currycomb appeared from one of the boy's apron pockets even before Phil and Kate had dismounted. Gerald was so deeply engrossed in his well-earned drink that Phil was certain the groom's hand on the bridle was completely unnecessary.

"You've had a good day, then." Not a question, a statement. A couple of pub patrons wandered out of the door, pints in hand, to observe the new arrivals.

"Fine, thanks." Phil wasn't expecting this opening conversational gambit and felt unsure how he ought to respond. The groom nodded and continued to brush the horse with long, smooth strokes.

"I'm Sean. This auld tippler likes his Guinness, so he does! If he was any quicker getting here from Patsy Slattery's, I'd be putting my wages on him to start winning races at the Curragh!" Sean said.

This drew a ripple of amusement from the bystanders, who reminded him that it would be a few years yet before he'd be allowed inside a bookmaker's office. Gerald had by now emptied the pail and licked it completely dry. An apple was produced from the depths of another apron pocket, and eagerly accepted.

Phil thought about offering to start releasing the buckles of the harness. He was stopped in his tracks by a voice behind him.

"Sure, the lad will sort that for you when he's finished grooming."

The speaker was a middle-aged man wearing a traditional striped apron. A clean, tidily folded towel hung from a belt around his slight paunch. Phil assumed this was the manager of the bar. "Michael Ashe?"

"The very same, and you'd be the couple from Patsy Slattery's stables down the road."

"That's right, Phil and Kate McDermott..."

For a few long seconds, time seemed to freeze. Phil noticed that everybody paused even in the raising or lowering of their respective glasses, and not a word was spoken. Finally, Michael Ashe seemed to shake himself and asked, "You're planning to stay down by the lakeside for a few days, Patsy's telling me?"

"Yes, that's right. I'm researching family history and we wanted a break."

"And how far has your research taken you?" Michael Ashe's eyes glistened.

Phil hesitated, suddenly reluctant to admit that their reason for making the journey lay in something as nebulous and insubstantial as a recurring dream. Some sort of answer, however, was required, and the landlord's open sincerity and interest encouraged him to open up far more than he normally would to a comparative stranger.

"I traced the family line for both my parents, and the Internet was a great help. I can't imagine how long it might have taken me if I'd had to trudge from one library or register office to the next searching for documents!"

He turned to hand Kate down from the box seat, and a gentle pressure from her fingertips confirmed that she had understood his verbal side-step. As Kate smoothed out her clothes, Phil turned back to Michael. "I'd like to refresh the glasses of those present, and add something for two thirsty travelers..."

The Chapel of Her Dreams

Paul Freeman

Paul McDermott
Nov 2024

Whimsical Publications, LLC

Florida

The Chapel of Her Dreams is a work of fiction. Names, characters, and incidents are the products of the author's imagination and are either fictitious or are used fictitiously. Any resemblance to actual events or persons, living or dead, is entirely coincidental.

If you purchased this book without a cover, you should be aware that this book may have been stolen property and reported as "unsold and destroyed" to the publisher. In such case, neither the publisher nor the author has received payment for this "stripped book."

Copyright © 2013 by Paul Freeman
All rights reserved

No part of this book may be reproduced in any form or by any electronic or mechanical means, including information storage and retrieval systems, without written permission from the publisher, except by a reviewer who may quote brief passages in a review.

To purchase the authorized electronic edition of The *Chapel of Her Dreams*, visit
www.whimsicalpublications.com

Cover art by Traci Markou
Editing by Brieanna Robertson

Published in the United States by
Whimsical Publications, LLC
Florida

ISBN-13: 978-1-936167-72-2

Printed in the United States of America

Acknowledgements

For KM, and the Dream we shared

Chapter 1

"Wake up, Kate. Wake up, it's alright, I'm here."

She opened her eyes; Phil continued to wipe her brow dry, and sat patiently with a glass of fresh water, which she accepted gratefully.

"Thought you'd need that. Same dream again?"

Kate nodded. Her throat was too dry. She dared not trust her voice until she had emptied the glass.

"Any more details?"

"I pushed the chapel door open this time, Phil. Why does it seem so familiar? It's as if I've visited the place, but at the same time...not," she ended lamely. She sat up and shook her hair from her face, frustrated at not being able to explain herself more clearly.

Phil nodded. They'd been over this ground a number of times already. Taking the empty glass, he used the distraction—and the slight noise—of replacing the glass on the bedside table to mask the discreet *click* of activating a tape recorder. Kate hated being taped, but he sensed it was important to record the details of her dream as accurately as possible.

"How about...outside the chapel? Still the same?"

"I come along a...a path through some woods, or a forest. It's not a paved road or anything. No, the chapel is definitely somewhere out in a....nature setting. There's some sort of an old, crumbly ruin behind it, but the chapel...it's almost as if it's untouched, somehow. Even untouchable...am I making sense?"

"Like, time has no effect on it, you mean?"

Kate nodded. Phil's sensitivity whenever she tried to describe her recurring dream, and any extra details she managed to remember, was something she had come to accept. Also, he had the knack of putting into words things that she sometimes found difficult to describe.

"It's almost as if—as if the chapel is the one 'real' thing, a photograph glued onto a sketch or a painted background—like a sort of a collage, you know?"

Phil knew exactly what she meant. It was a technique he often used in setting up displays of his freelance photography. "Care to try and sketch it for me?"

Kate reached for a pencil and began with a few firm strokes. Phil watched in fascination as the picture grew and took shape. He could never be jealous of Kate's artistic talents, which in many ways complemented his own musical skills, but there were times when he wished he could come even close to producing her lifelike sketches.

"Did you get any impression of how the chapel looks inside?"

They had discussed the dream many times, the way in which details seemed to become clear, like the gradual apparition of a photograph in a tray of developer, and with each repetition, they had both become more certain that the building and its location were real. They were also certain that neither of them had ever seen the chapel itself, or anything remotely resembling it.

After a brief pause to sort her impressions, Kate shook her head. "Not really, but there didn't seem to be any...what's the word, not benches..."

"Pews."

"Right, pews. I got the impression that the inside of the chapel was more or less empty, no pews, no altar, no furniture..."

"As if someone's stripped it, you mean?"

"No. At least, not if you mean do I think it's been sacked or vandalized. No, it sort of felt as if it was still a place of worship, but at the same time it felt...private, like a family chapel on an estate or something like that. The sort of place where you might not need lots of pews and statues and such." Kate's pencil hesitated seemingly of its own accord. With an abrupt movement, she laid it on the table. "Another brushstroke would spoil it," she said decisively.

Phil nodded agreement. In matters artistic, he trusted her judgement every time.

The chapel had definitive, solid, three-dimensional lines and contours. There was nothing vague or ill-defined about it. It had the feel of a still life sketch rather than something created from an artist's imagination.

For several moments, they both stared. The more they drank in, the more it took on a three-dimensional photographic quality.

"Know what?" said Phil. "That place is *real*. It *must* be possible to Google something to help us stick a pin in the map..."

It took three days of constant sifting through possible leads in every major search engine Phil could think of, but he found it at last. Kate came home to find him in front of the PC, gazing vacantly at an endlessly bouncing screensaver.

"Found it, and you're not going to believe what else I've found out!" were his first words.

"So try me." In all their years together, Kate had never seen the normally effervescent Phil in such a curious, reserved mood. Even when shattered after a long night getting something ready for an impossible deadline, he still had a smile or a joke on his lips.

His response, however, was totally unexpected. "Fancy a holiday?"

"What's that supposed to mean?"

He shook the computer mouse and a picture filled the screen.

Click. A computer-drawn image of Kate's sketch appeared in the top right corner of the picture. The enlargement of the photo was eerily close to Kate's apparently random design doodles.

Without comment, Phil boxed and enhanced a detail from the photograph just above the chapel door. Dragging it out, he enlarged it to fill about a quarter of the screen. Still without saying a word, he took Kate's original sketch from the worktop and held it next to the screen.

"What's that?" he asked.

It was unmistakable. The detail plucked from the photograph was identical in every respect with what had appeared at first glance to be free doodles and repeated motifs all over Kate's sketch. Kate glanced from the one to the other, thunderstruck.

"What...?"

"It's called a *triskele* design," explained Phil.

"No, that's not what I meant..."

"Sorry, Kate. I'm not trying to wind you up. I dredged a name for the design off the 'Net. I thought you as an artist might already know it..."

"Yes, you're right, I've heard the term before, but I'm at a loss to figure out why I've doodled it time and again all over the sketch. And look! It's even scribbled over the door, just about the same place you found it in the photo!"

Phil nodded. "That's what I thought, but I needed your confirmation to be certain. Want to know where it is?" Without waiting for an answer, he clicked the mouse again. The picture dissolved to a middle-distance shot of the same building, viewed from the same angle. Unmistakable ruins of a bigger, fortified castle surrounded by forest could be made out. Another *click* changed the perspective once more. The castle ruins were on an island. The picture appeared to have been taken from an airplane and formed an impressive upper right quadrant to...was it really an estate agent's brochure? Apparently it was.

Kate crouched closer to read for herself. She sat back a few seconds later, shaking her head. "Nice try, Phil, but I don't buy it! No way, José!"

"Honest, Kate, I didn't believe it either—but it checks out! Look, I've got a fistful of URLs. The estate agent's genuine."

She gave him one of her "looks," but he held his ground. Still unconvinced, she sat back from the screen and read once more. "Loch Cé, Co. Roscommon...island known as The Rock, Macdermot's Isle...is the ancestral home of... Phil, if you're winding me up..."

"Honest, sweetheart, it's so way out nobody would *dare* make it up!"

"And the crunch is—the island's for *sale*? Do people actually *buy* islands?"

"Apparently they do if they've a cool three-quarters of a mill to spare and they want a bit of privacy in Ireland! This estate agent must have an exclusive list of mega-rich clients. He seems to deal in nothing other than private islands and suchlike."

"Now tell me your Great-aunt Fanny's left you mega-bucks to pour into this hole in the ground!"

"No, but thanks for the idea! I must check if I've any rich relatives I could knock off and inherit from...much simpler, love! You know I've been thinking of researching my family tree for awhile now. Why don't we just...take off, do the Irish tourist bit, and head for that part of the world? You know you need a break, and we're not strapped for cash this month."

Before the day was over, flights had been found and booked.

"Thank God for budget airlines and standby tickets prices!" Phil hated parting with his hard-earned cash for any reason whatsoever.

Surfing to find quotes for car hire in Ireland—on the assumption that, since he had managed to get cut-price air tickets, this would work out cheaper than hiring a car and then paying for a ferry ticket—he stumbled on a local agent for a firm offering holiday packages in Ireland using horse-drawn, "gypsy-style" caravans. The idea appealed to both of them, and as there was a stable in a town called Boyle close to where they wished to go, he decided on a sudden impulse to book one for a fortnight. Kate had at least done some riding, and had some idea how to handle a horse, but as Phil said, "How hard can it be? I'll bet they're trained to stop every time they come to a pub!"

Packing never presented any terrors for Phil, who was used to being called out on short notice to photo shoots. He habitually travelled light. On working trips, he was just as likely to depart in the clothes he happened to be wearing, as long as he had a laptop, half a dozen cameras, and a credit card to cover everything else. Kate, the practical one, took charge of this aspect of their holiday.

"Do you realize," she said at one point as she snapped a case closed, "we haven't actually been away—I mean, *completely* away—not photo calls and business trips—for yonks!"

"Jeez, it must be 'yonks' since last time I heard anyone

use that word!" responded Phil, ducking automatically to avoid the cushion he knew would be tossed in his direction for the remark. Predictably, he ducked just in time and the cushion missed its mark.

"But listen!" he said, wisely changing the subject. "Did Slattery's say anything about whether we get a map of any sort? Because if not, perhaps I'd better be finding a decent OS map before we leave. It doesn't look more than about fifteen, maybe twenty miles from Boyle to the lake, but we'll need a large scale map of the area once we get there!"

A brief phone call to the agent's office was enough to ensure that a detailed OS map would be waiting for them when they collected the caravan.

Phil remained dubious as to how they would ever manage to wear the clothes packed into two full suitcases in a fortnight, but decided to hold his peace. Far more important as far as he was concerned were the two laptops and the selection of photographic and recording equipment he had selected as indispensable for his mission to trace what he privately thought of as The Chapel of Her Dreams.

Chapter 2

The flight from Liverpool to Knock was almost full, but Kate and Phil got to John Lennon Airport in good time, and were rewarded for their early arrival. Being near the front of the queue, they were able to claim two seats together near the front of the passenger cabin.

"Did you expect there to be this many people on an early morning flight?" Kate asked, looking at their fellow passengers. They appeared to be the only passengers under the age of about 50 or 60. Many of them were carrying—and using—rosary beads, but were not dressed in religious habits.

Phil glanced around and realized what had attracted Kate's attention.

"Knock is more than just a regional airport," he said. "I read about it on the 'Net. It's a place people go to on pilgrimage—like Lourdes in France."

Kate nodded, reassured to know that her fellow passengers were not terrified pessimists, pleading with the Almighty because the budget airline had a poor safety record.

In fact, the flight was smooth and uneventful. Less than an hour later, they rolled to a gentle stop at Knock Airport.

After a few unfortunate experiences, Phil had become close to paranoid about baggage handlers and cameras and insisted on carrying his equipment as cabin luggage. Privately, Kate thought he was probably right to think this way, and had no hesitation in applying the same "safety first" principle to their two laptops, without which she would have felt unable to function effectively.

Their main luggage safely reclaimed, they made their way through the concourse and headed for the local bus terminal. The pilgrims had filed onto a chartered coach, and they were left with a handful of other non-pilgrims traveling on the regular bus.

Some of them must be regulars, Phil realized, as the driver greeted them by name with a respectful familiarity. He was equally courteous when Phil and Kate arrived with their cases, taking them with an easy motion born of long practice. He stacked neatly in the baggage hold, in such a confident yet careful manner that Phil would not have been concerned if they had been full of priceless porcelain.

"Can you tell me what time you expect to get to Boyle?" asked Phil as he thanked the driver and bought their tickets for the penultimate stage of their journey.

"Now, whereabouts would you be staying?" The unhurried, cadenced lilt of his voice was all that a comedian would try to pass off as an amusing Irish brogue. This, on the other hand, was genuine.

"We've arranged to hire a caravan from Slattery's—"

"Ah! So it's the livery yard you'll be wanting. I can make a short stop and place you right outside them. It's before we go into the town center. Mrs. Heenan, you'll not mind the extra few minutes?"

Mrs. Heenan, already comfortably sitting near the driver's seat, allowed that she was in no hurry to get home; her daughter would have the tea on by that time, and how was Mrs. Doyle now? Phil soon gathered this inquiry concerned the health of the driver's wife.

The driver, Mike, winked at Phil and hinted that Mrs. Heenan would probably talk non-stop the whole trip, whether anyone listened to her or not. Silently, he looked his wristwatch and indicated that they could expect to reach Boyle at about one o'clock, aided or abetted by Mrs. Heenan's monologues.

Passengers got on and off the bus at no specific boarding points as far as Phil could see, but as most of them seemed to know each other well, he supposed this was just an aspect of the Irish *modus vivandi* he had heard gently satirized by one comedian after another throughout his life. Experiencing it now at first hand, he quickly formed the opinion that it was a way of life, which had much to commend it, and deserved better than the comic strip two-dimensional level of humor his earlier experiences had suggested.

There was no denying it. Life was lived at a slower pace in rural Ireland, but the bus driver seemed to have the road more or less to himself, apart from the occasional farm vehicle, and the clock was respectably close to one when Mike pulled into a layby, which boasted a bus timetable and a wooden shelter.

As he unloaded the suitcases, Mike said, "It wants a few minutes yet, but Patsy'll be along presently to drive you to the farmhouse." Seeing Phil's look of puzzlement, he added, "When you told me your destination, I rang ahead to Patsy Slattery. She said she'd meet the bus and drive you up to the stables...look, here she is now!"

A battered, muddy Land Rover bumped along the side road—little more than a rutted lane, really—which ran more or less at right angles to the two-lane tarmac from Knock to Boyle. The driver seemed to turn the vehicle almost in its own length to face back the way she had come. The engine sounded smooth, though, and chuffed quietly as Patsy Slattery came over to greet them and collect their luggage.

"Good afternoon to you both. I hope Mike's been driving a bit more carefully than he usually does, since he was carrying guests o' mine! I hope you've had a good trip, and you've room for a drop of tay when we get back."

By the time Patsy had greeted all and sundry, Mike had extracted Phil and Kate's luggage from the baggage area. Patsy left the bus as the cases were transferred to the Land Rover. "Thank you, Mike. Drive safely now!" were her final words as she waved a Mary Poppins-style parasol Kate hadn't noticed until now after the disappearing bus.

Once installed behind the wheel again, she seemed to downshift several gears and addressed Phil and Kate in a much calmer, unhurried fashion.

She had what Phil thought was an unnerving habit of using her hands as much as her voice in conversation, sometimes using both hands to illustrate a point, pressing a knee against the wheel if she deemed it necessary. However, on the short drive to the farm, he noticed that the ruts in the lane were quite deep, and the Land Rover was unlikely to bounce out of them even without the minimal guidance Patsy's hands could offer on the occasions they fluttered briefly

briefly on the steering wheel.

Mrs. Slattery's idea of "tay" when they arrived at the farm was vastly different to the frenetic, snatched half-cup of cool, insipid teabag infusion that was the day-to-day norm for both Phil and Kate.

A kettle bubbled invitingly on the hob—a genuine wood-burning range occupying most of one wall of the kitchen. Copious quantities of loose leaf tea, which Kate could not recall having seen anyone use in her quarter-century of existence, were measured into a large, brown ceramic teapot, which had been left to warm through on the corner of the range. She later confided to Phil that she had half expected the spoon she used to stir her drink with to dissolve in the brew.

The delicate aroma of the tea was overlaid by the distinctive and irresistible smell of freshly baked soda bread, mingled with other equally mouth-watering suggestions of scones, melting butter, and a selection of what were evidently home-made jams.

It had been some considerable time since the plastic rolls they had grabbed as grazing fodder at Liverpool Airport, and their digestive juices suddenly kicked into overdrive.

They needed no persuasion or encouragement to sit at the table, where Mrs. Slattery presided over the teapot and matched them slice for slice, biscuit for biscuit. Kate wondered at this, too. Granted, Patsy was obviously an outdoors person, glowing with good health, and well-proportioned with a tone of muscle that can only be achieved by regular exercise. However, she still appeared svelte rather than heavily built, and whatever calories she chose to pack away at a meal were clearly being burnt off between times.

Patsy also kept up a running conversation throughout the meal. Without appearing to pry, she successfully extracted from them many of the details of their reasons for visiting Ireland. Based on what they told her as they ate, she then provided—seemingly effortlessly and from memory—many useful snippets of information, which they might find they needed during their stay.

Like hobbits, they only left the table when it was starting to look somewhat bare.

"Sure, and it's good to see you young people getting a decent meal inside you fer once!" was all Patsy would say when they thanked her for her hospitality and tried to offer her a price for the banquet.

"We'll go and say hello to Gerald, now," she said when Phil insisted she take some money for her troubles.

"Sure, and he's the horse who'll be showing you around this part of God's Little Acre for the next two weeks!" she added when a look of puzzlement settled briefly on Phil's brow.

"And while I think, you're to tell that Michael Ashe at the Castle Inn that he'll have Patsy Slattery to answer to personally if he doesn't take good care of Gerald while he's up there. Tell him I'll sour his ale and stop his butter from setting in the churn, so I will!"

Neither Phil nor Kate was quite sure if Patsy was serious or not. Surely people didn't still claim to have the powers of witches, did they? Looking at the glint in Patsy's dark green-flecked eyes, Phil decided not to pursue the matter, but to take it at face value.

"I take it Michael Ashe is the landlord of the pub, and he knows you? Do you know if we can get meals at the pub? It would save us a lot of time."

"Young Michael knows Ma Patsy well enough, and he's got a half-decent cook last I heard so meals shouldn't be a problem —as long as you don't expect a pub to serve breakfast at some ungodly hour o' the morning!"

They had continued to walk alongside Patsy throughout this conversation and now found themselves suddenly opening one of a pair of double doors leading onto an open courtyard. Across the courtyard was a stable, complete with thatched roof.

A caravan, painted brightly in traditional reds and greens, stood ready, its shafts resting on the cobbles. Patsy's voice brought a nickering *"humph!"* from the open half door of the stall, and a wise-looking chestnut brown head appeared.

"Phil, he's *gorgeous*!" gasped Kate, picking up the tempo of her stride and automatically grasping in her pocket for a carrot or an apple, something with which to befriend their transport provider. Patsy seemed to be reading her thoughts and thrust an apple into her hand.

"Just this once, then, but don't spoil him *too* often or you'll have to bribe him twenty times a day to get any work out if him at all!"

Kate wondered for a moment if Patsy could read minds,

or if she really *was* the witch she hinted at being. On the other hand, she suspected that the vast majority of tourists arriving at the stables would have reacted in similar fashion. Patsy probably had an apple or something in her pocket every time she took someone out to the courtyard for precisely this reason.

It was by now mid-afternoon and Gerald seemed willing and eager to back into the shafts and walk about the courtyard and into an adjoining field whilst both Phil and Kate got a feel for sitting comfortably with reins in hand, nominally in control of the caravan.

"You'll find he has his little ways, but he's an experienced horse and he knows his way around," said Patsy when both Kate and Phil felt ready to depart.

"Does that mean he knows where to stop each night?" asked Kate.

He's covered a number of different routes from one campsite to another," replied Patsy. She paused a moment, and added, "He's been all around this part of Roscommon—or Moylurg, if you want to use the ancient name for the region, considering what you're looking into while you're here!"

"Moylurg?" Phil's ears pricked. This sounded like something interesting, something that might also be of value to their research.

"If you get time to sit and use those fancy computers you carry round, you can find out a lot about the ancient Kingdom of Moylurg, and the tale of Una Bahn and Tomàs is something else you should look into."

When pressed, she proclaimed herself too scatty to be of any use as a taleteller, a skill she quite clearly regarded as an art form beyond her own capabilities. She politely but steadfastly refused to be drawn, and insisted that they could get a far better rendering of the legend by surfing the 'Net.

Phil had to be content with that, but was quite happy to let Kate take first turn at the reins whilst he made the first searches into the fresh directions suggested by their host.

As late afternoon blurred into early evening, Kate sat on the comfortably broad driving ledge, reins held loosely in her hand. The main tourist season was singing its final verse, and they had hardly seen any traffic since leaving the livery yards. A golden westering sun approached the treetops, casting a steadily lengthening shadow before them. On either side of the road, honeysuckle plaited itself throughout the roadside hedges, trimmed back to just below their vantage point on the driving bench; the pungent scent of the flowers as they prepared to close themselves away for the evening was almost visible.

Phil appeared, carrying two steaming hot mugs of coffee and sat next to her. He glanced briefly at his watch then frowned. Placing the mug to one side, he stripped off his watch and thrust it into his trouser pocket.

Kate stared. In all the years she'd known Phil, she had only ever seen him take his watch off when swimming or showering, otherwise he wore it constantly, declaring he couldn't even sleep properly if he wasn't wearing it.

"I can't stand the idea of ever being late for something, anything at all!" he'd admitted once when she'd teased him about this. Now, however, he appeared to be breaking the habit of a lifetime, and she was at a momentary loss to understand why.

Phil spotted the look on her face and chuckled. "Livin' on Tulsa Time..." he quoted at her—another habit he had, of finding an appropriate song lyric from his memory banks to cover just about any occasion. Kate waited patiently. Sometimes the reasons for his choice of lyric weren't immediately obvious to her.

"Yeah, well, it seems to me that the pace of life is so much different here! A calendar is more useful than a wristwatch. We don't want to lose track of the date and forget to take Gerald back home on the right day now, do we?"

Kate grinned and toasted him with her coffee mug. "Phil, you don't know how much I've been wanting to see you slow down and relax a bit more. You've really driven yourself far too hard these last few months, you know? If anyone deserves a *real* slow-down, get-off-the-motorway type of holiday, it's you!"

"Tell you what, sweetheart, the only clock I'm taking any notice of the next few days is the biological one that lets me know when I should eat...drink...and..."

"And everything else, yes, thanks, I get the picture! Look, is that a pub ahead?"

"Gerald seems to think so; he's almost breaking out into a...a fast walk, I suppose you'd call it!"

Phil's less than complimentary description of Gerald's

speed was a little bit unfair, but if truth were to be told, not by very much. Gerald was definitely getting long in the tooth, but good for a few more years of tourism before a well-earned retirement field beckoned.

The hand-crafted sign outside the pub stated without fuss the patently obvious fact that this was indeed Michael Ashe's Pub, their first night's scheduled stop. Even before they drew onto the forecourt, a young lad of at least thirteen or fourteen appeared from somewhere behind the pub, wearing a leather apron and carrying a metal pail.

The pail hit the ground immediately in front of Gerald's eager muzzle; a currycomb appeared from one of the boy's apron pockets even before Phil and Kate had dismounted. Gerald was so deeply engrossed in his well-earned drink that Phil was certain the groom's hand on the bridle was completely unnecessary.

"You've had a good day, then." Not a question, a statement. A couple of pub patrons wandered out of the door, pints in hand, to observe the new arrivals.

"Fine, thanks." Phil wasn't expecting this opening conversational gambit and felt unsure how he ought to respond. The groom nodded and continued to brush the horse with long, smooth strokes.

"I'm Sean. This auld tippler likes his Guinness, so he does! If he was any quicker getting here from Patsy Slattery's, I'd be putting my wages on him to start winning races at the Curragh!" Sean said.

This drew a ripple of amusement from the bystanders, who reminded him that it would be a few years yet before he'd be allowed inside a bookmaker's office. Gerald had by now emptied the pail and licked it completely dry. An apple was produced from the depths of another apron pocket, and eagerly accepted.

Phil thought about offering to start releasing the buckles of the harness. He was stopped in his tracks by a voice behind him.

"Sure, the lad will sort that for you when he's finished grooming."

The speaker was a middle-aged man wearing a traditional striped apron. A clean, tidily folded towel hung from a belt around his slight paunch. Phil assumed this was the manager of the bar. "Michael Ashe?"

"The very same, and you'd be the couple from Patsy Slattery's stables down the road."

"That's right, Phil and Kate McDermott..."

For a few long seconds, time seemed to freeze. Phil noticed that everybody paused even in the raising or lowering of their respective glasses, and not a word was spoken. Finally, Michael Ashe seemed to shake himself and asked, "You're planning to stay down by the lakeside for a few days, Patsy's telling me?"

"Yes, that's right. I'm researching family history and we wanted a break."

"And how far has your research taken you?" Michael Ashe's eyes glistened.

Phil hesitated, suddenly reluctant to admit that their reason for making the journey lay in something as nebulous and insubstantial as a recurring dream. Some sort of answer, however, was required, and the landlord's open sincerity and interest encouraged him to open up far more than he normally would to a comparative stranger.

"I traced the family line for both my parents, and the Internet was a great help. I can't imagine how long it might have taken me if I'd had to trudge from one library or register office to the next searching for documents!"

He turned to hand Kate down from the box seat, and a gentle pressure from her fingertips confirmed that she had understood his verbal side-step. As Kate smoothed out her clothes, Phil turned back to Michael. "I'd like to refresh the glasses of those present, and add something for two thirsty travelers..."

When it could no longer be denied that the light was draining from the sky, Phil started to wonder about how they were going to find their way to the lakeside where they planned to park the caravan. He hadn't held back from drinking—after all, he had no intention of driving anywhere—but he was sober enough to think about practical matters.

An evening meal, which he had no memory of having ordered, had appeared and been swiftly dispatched. The pub had filled with more drinkers as the evening had progressed, and most of them had stayed to greet the travelers. A group waiting to be served had started singing, and within minutes, an impromptu concert party had been formed. Kate had fallen into conversation with a local artist, a girl of about her own age. They had been comparing sketches, techniques and other "arty-farty" matters completely outside Phil's field of knowledge, and looked likely to continue doing so unless they were physically separated.

He drained his glass and wove his way between stools toward the bar. Michael Ashe was already filling a replacement Guinness, topping it off with a stylised shamrock as Phil arrived.

"I think we'll have to ask for directions to the lake after this one," he began.

Michael smiled, shaking his head. "Sure, and I told Jim to stable old Gerard for the night. You can sleep in the caravan where it is and I'll follow you down after breakfast tomorrow!"

Truth to tell, Phil had been reluctant to leave the friendly, good-natured crowd and the excellent Guinness, so he had no hesitation in accepting Michael's most practical of solutions. He took his own drink and Kate's, made sure Michael had one himself, and bought a round for the quartet of singers who coincidentally ended a number just as he was about to pay. As an afterthought, he glanced over to where Kate was sitting and added a glass of red wine for the girl sitting with her, whose name he hadn't quite caught.

"Don't you have licensing hours here?" he asked, more in idle curiosity than because he really needed to know.

Michael nodded over toward the corner. "D'ye see the big fella singing bass?"

Phil nodded. The singer was easy to identify. He was almost as stout as he was tall, and with the reddest complexion Phil had ever seen, he had a remarkably true voice.

"That's our local bobby!" crowed Michael, exploding into laughter. "So if anyone gets a bit 'frisky,' he'll soon sort them out!"

"And how about closing time? When do you close?"

Michael made a solemn show of consulting his wristwatch. "September!" he said, and exploded once more into laughter. Several of those standing closest to the bar had obviously heard the joke before, as they joined Michael in shouting out the name of the month in unison. Grinning his appreciation to show that he didn't mind being played for the "fall guy" in this little exchange, Phil made his way back to their table.

"What was that all about?" Kate wanted to know as he hovered over the table, looking for a space big enough to deposit three glasses. Phil explained, and raised a few encore grins from both girls.

"Phil, this is Moira...is that M-o-i-r-a, the way my friend spells it?"

"That's right, though I understand why you're a bit wary of the way some of the older, traditional Irish names are spelled!"

"She saw my file poking out of the bag, and my secret's out!" laughed Kate. "She's off to art college in Dublin soon, and she was admiring my sketches. She's asked me to look at some of her local scenes tomorrow, if that's alright with you?"

"Why would I mind? You're the artist, not me. And after all, it's not as if we're working to a tight deadline or anything like that."

"Now, what did I tell you?" crowed Kate "Whenever I need something for my art work, nothing's too much trouble. Do you have someone to help you out, Moira?"

Moira looked from one to the other as she took the fresh glass of wine from the tray Phil carried. "Thanks for the drink. There was really no need, you know. Kate, my 'significant other,' as I suppose you'd call him, is already in Dublin, enrolled at the same college. He's a year or so older than me."

Phil sipped at his drink, automatically licking away the cream from his upper lip.

"Has he sold anything, or is he studying full time? I don't mean to pry, but it's a fact that your chosen field is a minefield of financial disasters waiting to happen. What I suspect Kate's trying to say is that you'll find there are times when a steady, reliable source of income will be vital—and there aren't many art students who have that."

"Peter's got some money behind him—the family's not *loaded*, but...he has a bit of independence, I suppose, and he's sold some work from time to time. He's on a scholarship from a firm who has a position for him once he qualifies. Some sort of graphic designer, he told me."

"Have you started to put a portfolio together, Moira? And have you any special interests?" Kate asked, chafing slightly to get back to the technical matters they'd been discussing while Phil was at the bar.

Moira took a generous gulp from her glass.

"I've concentrated on local landscapes, black and white sketching for the most part. They're cheaper than pastels or watercolors." Suddenly, she pounced on one of the sketches in Kate's file. "Didn't I see you arrive here only this afternoon? You haven't had time to..." Her voice trailed off uncertainly.

Kate glanced at the sketch Moira was holding up, and immediately looked to Phil.

Phil cleared his throat. "You're right about us only arriving this afternoon, about four o'clock, I think it was. Mrs. Slattery said we should take it easy and not try to go too far on the first day."

He half-stood to peer over Moira's shoulder at the sketch that had caught her attention.

"Kate hasn't made any sketches since we arrived," he said. He then recognized the picture in question, and felt an adrenaline jolt play havoc with his heartbeat for several seconds.

"That's a sketch of something she's seen several times in a...series of dreams," he said, quietly. "Do you recognize something in it?"

Moira didn't answer at once, but looked in the direction of the bar. Phil happened to be facing that direction already. At that distance, Michael Ashe couldn't possibly have heard Phil's words, but he spun round as if stung on the back of his neck, caught Moira's eye, and came over to join them at once.

"Tell Phil and Kate where they'll find this, would you, Michael?"

"Moira, that's as fine a sketch of the chapel on The Rock as I've seen you do yet! But this is a close-up, surely? I didn't know you'd rowed out to it..."

"Michael, it's not *my* sketch."

"Kate drew it last week in Liverpool when she woke from a dream," Phil offered when Moira, for some reason, seemed reluctant to complete the sentence.

"We'll speak after hours, in private, if you'll not mind,"

said Michael quietly, "though I've a feeling that might not be too far off now."

The concert party grouped around the hearth had full glasses and now stood in a more formal pose than previously facing the Irish tricolor, which was draped above a number of photographs and other memorabilia on display. Conversation stilled, and everyone in the bar stood and faced the same direction.

A keen Rugby fan, Phil had heard the Irish national anthem sung many times before international matches. In reality, he supposed it must have registered on each occasion that he had not been able to make out what language was being sung, but this was the first time he had heard the Gaelic lyrics clearly. Naturally, he understood not a word, but the bitter-sweet feeling of the melody affected him emotionally nevertheless. As it ended and people emptied their glasses and bade each other, "God bless and good night," he sensed that he had been privileged to witness a unique aspect of rural Irish society.

Most of the evening's patrons had taken the trouble to deposit their glasses on the bar as they left. Phil, Kate, and Moira helped Michael to set the room to rights and collected the odd stray glasses. Jim, the stable lad, apparently doubled as potboy, and it wasn't long before every glass had been cleaned, polished, and stored back in its rightful place.

Wiping his hands on yet another pristine, laundered towel, Michael reached without looking under the counter and produced a green bottle without label. This he placed on a tray with half a dozen shot glasses, and cuffed Jim on his way.

"Mind you go straight to bed, now, this is adult business!" he growled. All the same, he waited until he heard evidence of Jim's boots on the wooden stairway to the upper floor before he went round and sat at the table now occupied by Phil, Kate, and Moira.

He looked from one to another then seemed to come to some sort of decision. As he poured carefully into each glass, he addressed his opening remarks directly to Moira. "Moira, if I hadn't known you as long as I have, and been as certain as

I can be that you're incapable of telling a lie, I'd not believe that this picture could possibly be the work of someone who's never sat on the banks of Loch Cé and sketched what was right there in front of them! Kate, Phil, what can I say to you? You know that you bear the name, and that your family's roots are deeper here in what's now called Roscommon than anywhere else. *Slàinthe!*" He raised his glass. The others followed suit automatically.

Moira clearly knew what they were being offered, and Phil watched carefully, noting how she took a *very* small sip at her glass; he opted to do the same. He was still surprised at the sheer potency of the drink, but managed to avoid being taken by surprise and spluttering. Kate took her cue from Phil, and just about managed to keep her breathing under control.

Michael smiled, and Phil sensed that they had just passed some sort of test. Michael rose from his seat, refilled their shot glasses with more of the *poteen,* and returned to the bar to "top up" chaser glasses of Guinness, which Phil hadn't noticed being started.

"Let me have another look at that sketch if you would, Kate...thanks. Would you mind giving Moira a sheet or two from your sketch pad and lend her a pencil?"

For several long moments, Michael studied the sketch closely.

"Moira, can you sketch from memory the chapel seen from the lakeside, from about the same...angle, or whatever you artist types call it?"

Moira nodded and quickly roughed out a perspective of a building that was clearly the same chapel. It was viewed from the same vantage point, but from a further distance. This was brought out by a suggestion of water and some coastline in the chapel's immediate foreground.

Michael looked at it, nodded, and placed Moira's sketch alongside Kate's. Allowing for differences in scale, it was immediately obvious that they were renderings of the same building. Phil always claimed he had no artistic sense whatsoever, but as a professional photographer—and a *good* one—he was also convinced that there could be no doubt.

"There's just one thing," Michael murmured, tapping first the one sketch then the other. "Kate, why does the building in your sketch look...more complete, or less damaged if you'd rather think of it like that?"

Kate had no answer to this. Phil shrugged. "That's just how Kate 'sees it' in her dream, a dream she has more and more often recently. It's been disturbing her so much she's been having difficulty sleeping, and that's one of the reasons we decided to take this holiday."

"What, like a sort of *Ghostbusters* vacation, you mean? To try and 'lay the ghost' and get some peace?" Though in certain circumstances, this might have sounded trite, flippant, or even somewhat offensive, Moira's sincerity was unmistakeable.

Kate nodded. "That just about says it all, Moira. We'd enough put by to be able to take an unscheduled holiday, also we're both freelancers and don't have to ask a boss for permission to take a break. For the moment, most of the commission work in hand can be done through a PC anywhere in the world. That's why we can be here just when it suits us."

Moira nodded. Her attention was still, however, centered on the two drawings. "When you see the chapel in daylight tomorrow, you'll appreciate why Michael's puzzled by your...rendering, I suppose would be a good term, compared with what it actually looks like *today*, which is in fact much closer to the remains, or ruins, as they appear in my sketch. I'd say that your sketch looks much as I imagine it would have looked some time ago, quite a *long* time ago, in fact!"

Moira's casual comment caused both Kate's and Phil's ears to prick. For them, this was a significant snippet of information that dovetailed with what they already knew. For the first time, Phil sensed he could see a pattern developing.

"Are you saying Kate's sketch looks like a...historically earlier version?" he asked.

Michael leaned across the table. "If it's earlier records of the chapel you're looking for, I can tell you of the earliest story connected with it."

Phil's fingers itched. Surely here was a tale that could be very important and might even have some relevance to his research into family links. "Michael, do you mind if I record this story? It may help with my family research..."

Michael nodded his agreement, and Phil sprinted out of the door. When he returned from the caravan, he discovered that Michael had refilled everyone's glasses—both the larger and the smaller—and the group had decamped from the table to a more comfortable, informal setting in easy chairs grouped around the open turf fire.

"The tale of Una Bhan, daughter to Cormac, King of Moylurg and her would-be suitor Tomàs Laidir Costello, is well-known in these parts. It is as true as it is tragic," Michael began, staring into the dancing flames as if this helped him concentrate on the words. "Una Bhan was very beautiful, and had extremely long, fine blonde hair, which cascaded down her back almost to her knees. Cormac was proud of her, as any father might be, yet as king, he felt he had a duty to vet all her would-be suitors. None of them were ever good enough to satisfy him.

"One was a close neighbor, a handsome and affluent young man whose affections were sincere. Cormac, however, considered Tomàs not good enough for his beloved daughter, and had her confined to The Rock, as Trinity Isle was often called at the time. Tomàs was banished from the area. Una Bhan sickened from day to day, falling into a melancholy, and lay dying of grief. Tomàs heard of the situation and went to see her, in defiance of Cormac's ban. When he left, he vowed that unless Cormac sent word that he might return before he reached the river that marked the boundaries between their estates, he would never come back. Cormac repented, and word was sent, but it did not reach Tomàs until after he had crossed the river. Being a man of honor, he held to his word and refused to return.

"Una Bhan died of a broken heart and was buried on Trinity Isle. In his grief, Tomàs used to swim out to keep vigil at her grave every night. Eventually, he caught pneumonia. Realizing he was dying, he requested of Cormac that he be buried alongside Una Bhan. His request was granted. Tradition says that two rose trees grew from the lovers' graves, entwining above them, and can still be seen today."

The spell woven by Michael's recital of this tale created an atmosphere of peace. Several seconds of contemplative silence ended with a sudden crackle and flare from the turf fire as it burned lower and settled under its own weight.

Moira shuddered. "You tell the tale well, Michael. I'm thinking a goose just walked over my grave!"

Kate looked nonplussed at this remark, but Phil thought he could guess the sense of it, as he consciously willed the hairs on the back of his neck into place.

Michael stirred in his seat. "I simply repeat the story as it was told to me. You'll have to check somewhere else for exact dates, but Cormac an MacDairmada and Tomàs Laidir Costello are both historical figures and you'll find plenty of references to both in written records."

"So you're saying that Kate has somehow captured in her sketches the...the 'spirit' of what the chapel *may* have looked like, what, a hundred years ago? More?"

"There was a 'folly' built on the site of the castle some time in the eighteen hundreds that was burnt down just before the last World War," replied Michael. "But the original building dates from much earlier, at least four hundred years ago, and probably more."

Phil had been tapping on his laptop, snatched from the caravan almost as an afterthought when he had gone back for the tape recorder.

"That wasn't the first fire, either, according to this site. The castle was literally bombed into submission in twelve-thirty-five by fireships, and an earlier building burned down after being struck by lightning a hundred years before that!"

Kate's brow furrowed with concern. "You know what you're like, Phil. Let's not get sidetracked. What we're trying to find out is a reason for the differences between my sketches and Moira's. The history of the castle may have something to do with it, but as yet, we're still no closer to an explanation of this."

Sighing, Phil punched a shortcut key, saving the page he'd been scanning into Favorites for future reference. With obvious reluctance, he broke the 'Net connection.

"How much can you tell us of local history, Michael?" Kate asked.

Michael appeared embarrassed at the question. "Well, now, I'm what you'd call a newcomer," he began, but Moira interrupted.

"Michael Ashe, you've lived in this village more than my twenty-odd summers and you know it!" She turned to Kate and Phil. "What Michael means is that there are others in the village who are older, have never left the village all their lives, and know more of the gossip and traditions of Roscommon than he does; though as innkeeper, he probably knows more *about* certain people and their secrets than they're likely to feel comfortable with!"

Michael had the decency to blush at this, and Moira pressed home her advantage. "Michael, why don't you have a word with Hugh O'Gara tomorrow morning? He's just the sort of person who'd know more than anyone else about this sort of thing."

The turf was now reduced to dying embers, and there was little or nothing left in anyone's glass. Glasses were washed and put away, and Michael was thanked again for his hospitality. Moira led Phil and Kate across the courtyard to the parked caravan and made sure they negotiated the steps safely before she wished them God bless and good night and continued down the road into the village proper.

Chapter Three

Phil had always been an early riser, surviving happily on three to four hours sleep. Despite his vow not to be ruled by his wristwatch during their holiday, he was up and experimenting with the Calor gas stove at first light. As the kettle came to the boil, he poured it over a generous portion of fresh-ground Kenyan beans and left it to percolate. The tantalizing aroma of the day's first brew soon produced a reaction from Kate.

"Wassatime?"

"Morning. I told you, my watch is in the 'sin bin' for the next few weeks."

"Zat coffee?"

"It isn't diesel oil."

"Mmmm, your coffee's always good. What are your plans today?"

"Breakfast, and then before we go down to the lake, we should look after old Gerald. He might not be dragging a caravan X miles every day, but we still need to look after him."

"Sure, but that's no great hardship. Actually, I think I'm going to enjoy it. I always wanted to own a horse when I was a kid."

"You and just about every girl in England, I'm sure," chuckled Phil, tousling her untameable hair with a free hand. He glanced out the rear door, the top half of which he had fastened back. Michael Ashe showed himself at the front door of the pub and waved to them to come over to the kitchen.

"I think breakfast might be ready," Phil added.

Kate roused herself, washed, and dressed quickly. The unpolluted country air had undoubtedly quickened her appetite. As they entered the kitchen, Michael drew out two chairs from the table in the center of the room. A traditional wood-burning kitchen range occupied most of one wall, and a series of pots and pans bubbled or simmered on it.

There were four place settings; Moira joined Phil, Kate, and Michael as she deposited the last few dishes in the center of the table.

"I hope you've brought your appetites with you," she said with a mock frown.

"If you take a decent breakfast, you'll not lose time stopping for a lengthy lunch," added Michael, setting a good example by filling his plate.

"Sure, and the *liquid* element of lunches, in my experience, is what causes most delay!" Moira added, tartly but without malice.

Kate's idea of breakfast was generally more on the lines of two or three coffees and a slice of toast, but the fresh air had given her a healthy appetite, too.

Phil had no inhibitions and set about the "Full Irish Breakfast" provided by Michael Ashe with enthusiasm.

Kate insisted on helping Moira with the dishes, protesting that this was surely the least she could do to show their appreciation. Phil used the time to go through his collection of cameras and equipment.

By the time Kate returned to the caravan, Phil had made his selections, and they went together to feed and brush Gerard. The stable lad, Phil remembered Moira calling him Jim, appeared from nowhere and helped them to back the horse in between the shafts for the short trip to the lakeside and the campsite that would be their center of operations for the next fortnight or so.

Moira appeared at the kitchen door just as they were ready to go. Leaning heavily on her arm was an elderly man, not a face which Phil could immediately place from the previous night's festivities. By now, it was almost time for Michael Ashe to open for business. The postman had already enjoyed his regular swift tipple before completing his local delivery round.

Moira's companion, Phil sensed, moved slowly due to his

considerable age, but there was still an air of strength and authority about him. Without being able to explain why, Phil instinctively knew that this was, in all likelihood, the village's oldest inhabitant, or Elder Statesman; the official-sounding title almost begged to be spelled with capital letters.

"Phil, Kate, this is Hugh O'Gara. You may recall he was mentioned last night as our local expert on just about everything that's ever happened in the village of Ardcarne. He's probably forgotten more than the rest of us ever learned!"

Hugh's grasp on Phil's hand was surprisingly strong, and confirmed Phil's instinctive feeling that this was indeed a figure of genuine authority.

"I'm informed that you're searching through your family's history," Hugh said calmly.

"How far have your labors taken you?"

"It's been fairly simple, actually," began Phil, "because my father, Terry, had only me and I've no close male cousins. The same's true of his father, though there's been any number of girls in both generations! His father was—"

"Tomàs McDermott, who had any number of brothers and male cousins!" interrupted Hugh. His eyes sparked with satisfaction as he saw Phil's reaction. He nodded, and continued. "Tomàs McDermott, his brothers, and his cousins were a well-known local team. They traveled together playing exhibition Rugby and Hurling matches depending on the time of year against any opposition. From all accounts, they lost very few of their games!

"Like many of their generation, they were obliged to leave when the crops failed three years running. The O'Gara family had always been tenants on the Clan McDermott estate, but we had no money of our own and were obliged to remain. But I'm not as old as all that. The tale I'm telling you is one I heard from my grandfather, who watched them as a team many times when he was young!"

Phil saw at once that this village resident's memories could prove invaluable to his researches. Fortunately, Hugh seemed not only willing, but also eager to contribute.

Kate and Moira wandered off ahead of the caravan, leading the way. Hugh declined the offer of a ride on the principle that "It would take me half an hour to get up and longer, no doubt, to get back down again." So he and Phil strolled alongside Gerald, the reins being held by an ecstatically hap-

happy Jim on the box seat.

The pub was barely concealed by the thinnest screen of leaves and foliage when they arrived at a natural clearing, complete with a combined picnic table and benches. It was located at the extreme southernmost tip of the teardrop-shaped lake and seemed to be a perfect place for their campsite. Less than thirty meters from the bank was the closest point of an island, and the unmistakeable lines of what could only have been a chapel. This confirmed that they had arrived at the island they sought, an isle which he had heard referred to under at very least a triumvirate of names: Castle Island, Trinity Isle, and McDermott's Isle—four, if you also counted The Rock. This, however, seemed to be more of a local name rather than something official recorded on an OS or tourist map.

Following Hugh's advice, the caravan was backed up to a point on the perimeter of the clearing furthest away from the water's edge and more or less opposite the picnic table. Gerald was unharnessed and left tethered away from both caravan and dining area.

"Michael will show you later where he can roam more freely in a pasture," said Hugh.

"Jim, when you go back, remind him of that, please, and when you get a moment, run over and tell Sean I want him."

Jim nodded and ran off.

"Sean's my grandson," explained Hugh, in response to Phil's unspoken question. "I thought to ask him to run a few errands for me, my legs not being up to it these days!"

Kate had already perched on a convenient tree stump and opened up her sketchpad. Moira hovered at her shoulder. At that distance, Phil could not overhear what was being said, but assumed they were discussing the production of some preliminary sketches.

"You've lost your good lady for awhile, I'm thinking," commented Hugh.

Phil grinned. "Isn't it always the way? But she's an artist, and in such a beautiful spot..." Phil trailed off, but the sentence didn't really need finishing.

"Don't let me stop you from setting up cameras and equipment," Hugh said, nodding his understanding. "You've no doubt your own preparations to make."

Grinning self-consciously, Phil began to unpack. "Hugh,

your knowledge and your memories would be a great help for me," he said.

"It would save me weeks of research if I could ask for your help."

"Haven't I already told you that the O'Garas have always been loyal to the clan?" said Hugh. "I took it for granted that you'd ask, and if you hadn't mentioned it yourself, I'd have offered before the day was much older. Of course you can count on me."

Phil was relieved. Despite the confidence he showed in his professional dealings, he was essentially a reserved, almost shy person where more personal matters were concerned. He thanked Hugh sincerely, thinking as he did so that mere words seemed inadequate.

"Where do you suggest I can set up a camera for a series of photographs?" he asked.

"A series? What sort of series d'you mean? And what for?"

"When I go somewhere I haven't been before, I like to start with a set of pictures of the scene. I find it useful if I can take a full set of the scene under different lighting conditions, so I try to set up a timer to take shots at regular intervals throughout the day, every half-hour, for example."

"That sounds like a lot of film. It must be expensive?"

Phil laughed. "Not if you do your own processing. It's only about two rolls, really. But that's one thing I'd like to ask, by the way. There isn't a photographer or a chemist in the village. Does Michael Ashe have a spare room at the pub I could rent?"

"I'm sure that can be arranged," Hugh said with a nod. "Is it really that simple to develop pictures?"

"If you know what you're doing, it's pretty straightforward," said Phil. "People just think it's complicated because the equipment's a bit pricey, but all you need really is a dark room and a few chemicals."

There was rather more skill involved than that, but like any true professional, Phil wasn't about to reveal any trade secrets. Hugh called Sean over and told him what Phil needed to know, sending him off toward the pub with a playful cuff. Within ten minutes, he was back with a positive answer and towing a crate of Guinness balanced on a shopping trolley.

"Michael says to keep them cool in the lake, and you can pay for what you drink when you get back."

Phil chose three strategic points on the shoreline, covering about ninety degrees from roughly a south-easterly point clockwise round to about south-west. What had been the chapel entrance faced as near as made no difference due south, according to Phil's compass. Once the cameras were in place and the timers set, his work for the afternoon was completed. He would return just before sundown to replace the films with specially sensitive film for night shots without the distortion of a flashgun.

Kate and Moira had also drifted from one vantage point to another, and had produced a score or more sketches. Most of them were Kate's handiwork, but Moira had produced a couple of creditable efforts as well. Phil and Hugh took the final two bottles of Guinness from the crate.

"Well begun is half-done!" Hugh intoned with a mock-solemn wink.

For some reason, this aphorism struck them all as hilarious, though the amount of Guinness consumed during the afternoon might also have had something to do with their good humor. Laughing and joking, they strolled back to the pub for their evening meal, more than satisfied with the results of the first day's labors.

Chapter 4

After a leisurely meal, washed down with suitable quantities of alcohol, Kate and Moira began comparing notes from their afternoon sketches. Soon there were sketches littering three or four tables as the two artists looked through their efforts.

Hugh O'Gara wandered across and glanced through the nearest stack, which appeared to be all Kate's work. Suddenly, he stiffened and extracted a single sheet of paper. "You've a very good eye for detail, young lady!" he said, placing the sketch in front of Kate and tapping at it with a fingertip. "Could you really see that tiny little...whatever it's called...at a distance of, what, it has to be thirty yards?"

Puzzled, Kate bent for a closer look. Her brows knit together.

"That's an older sketch, Hugh. I didn't even do that one today. It must be...oh, at least two weeks ago if not more. What d'you mean, though? What detail?"

Hugh tapped the page again. There was a recurring *motif* in doodles around the edge of the page, as if Kate had been practicing to get the shape she wanted before including it as a decoration above what appeared to be a door on the chapel:

"If you could see that...shape..."

"It's called a *triskele*, Hugh," she said.

"Thank you. Anyway, if you could see that...tree-skay-lay from where you were sitting, you've got eyes like the proverbial eagle!" he said with a grin.

Kate flushed. "Eagle. Well, Phil would have found a more down-to-earth expression," she muttered.

"Even so, if you're sure it's something you sketched even before you came to Ireland, it's even more remarkable," Hugh continued. "I can tell you, whatever it's called, you'll find it's as close as I can recall *exactly* a detail you'll see carved into the lintel of the door."

Phil leaned across to study it closely. Thinking of how Kate's dreams had been one of the main reasons for them making time for the trip in the first place, he felt a frisson of anticipation. Could this be a sign that his decision to follow a whim and come on this trip might just bear fruit? "I should be able to get some good close-up shots of that door and lintel. It's the main door you're talking about, isn't it, Hugh?"

"'Tis indeed."

"Thanks. The ground looked to be clear. I can set up a tripod overnight. Is there any chance someone could row me out there to take a few shots this afternoon while the light's still good?"

Sean was dispatched to find Jim, proud owner of the nearest available rowboat. Phil disappeared into the caravan to choose what he thought would be the best camera for the job in hand.

When Sean returned, practically dragging Jim with him, the courtyard was a hive of activity. However, when they reached the glade, its essential peace and tranquillity was undisturbed.

The rowboat was moored in a reedbed off to one side of the glade. Phil was a little surprised he hadn't noticed it earlier on, but on the other hand, he hadn't actually been looking for it. Sean took a seat in the prow without waiting for an invitation.

As soon as they had crossed the short distance to the island, Sean hopped out and helped Phil to secure the skiff from floating off without making it too difficult to re-launch.

He then took from Phil the various padded bags containing a selection of the camera paraphernalia deemed necessary for close-up photography. Phil melted to the silent puppy-dog-eyed plea in Sean's gaze when the equipment had been safely deposited on the shore, and after a swift glance in Hugh's direction, agreed that Sean might accompany him on his "photo safari."

"Let me carry your case, so you've got two hands free."

It was on the tip of Phil's tongue to refuse this undoubtedly well-meant offer, but something stopped him. Sean was, after all, a sturdy lad. He was agile and anxious to please, and had already shown that he was both reliable and swift in running errands. Perhaps he ought to cut the boy some slack, he thought.

"Okay, Sean, I could certainly use an extra pair of hands—but *careful* hands!" he added.

"Careful it is, sir," promised Sean gravely.

For the next twenty minutes or so, Sean followed Phil as obediently as an acolyte would a visiting Archbishop. As the daylight began to leak away, Phil passed Sean the camera he had used for the last set of close-ups he intended to take himself and began to assemble the first of several tripods for timed exposure shots through the night. After all, he mused, one never knew.

Sean's eyes grew bigger and rounder as he looked on in disbelief. "How many cameras d'yis need, sir?"

Phil realized that to a young boy, it must seem excessive. He had found in his day-to-day professional work that it was best to treat children and adults equally. In his opinion, there was no mileage in patronizing young people; therefore, he treated Sean's question seriously. "Taking photographs is my job, Sean," he explained. "And while I might not need all these, it's a sort of a habit for me to have them all handy, just in case, so to speak. I'd prefer to have one camera around and not need it rather than not have *exactly* what I need if something unexpected happens. Does that make sense to you?"

Sean nodded.

"I like taking pictures, too. Is it a good job? Could I do it when I'm older, sir?"

"Why not?" said Phil, without a trace of mockery or platitude. "I wasn't much older than you when I decided I wanted to be a photographer, but please, I'm not a 'sir.' That's best kept for when you go back to school after the holidays!"

"Sure, and I can't be calling you for your Christian name!" Sean protested with horror. "You're not just an adult, you're also a *guest*. And you're *a MacDairmada!*"

To calm the boy's evident distress, Phil sat down on the ground before him and waited until he had Sean's full attention. "Now, while there's just you and me, I want you to tell me a few things, young Sean." Placing one hand on Sean's shoulder, he brought him round to sit alongside him on a convenient stone. "From what Hugh O'Gara said last night, I've a good idea what *a MacDairmada* means. It's a traditional title for the head of the family, and he seems to think I've a claim to the title."

"It's more like Clan Chief, really," Sean interrupted. "It's more than just 'family,' really, even if it's just a title these days."

"Tell you what," Phil said. "Let's settle for another 'honorary' title, which I'd like you to use. Everyone's made Kate and me so welcome, you've made us feel like family. Why don't you call me Uncle Phil? That's got a nice, friendly ring to it, don't you think?" Sean's eyes flickered briefly to a point over and beyond Phil's shoulder, and Phil sensed that Sean was looking toward Hugh O'Gara, visible on the shore, but at the moment, out of earshot.

"And if you're thinking Hugh O'Gara's approval might be needed, I'll speak to him myself as soon as you paddle me back to the shore."

The relief on Sean's face was evident. With a nod and a bound, he was back on his feet and into the skiff, waiting for Phil to pass him the cameras and accessories that were not needed for the night shots.

Back at Michael Ashe's Inn, after Sean had been dispatched back to his family, Hugh listened carefully as Phil gave him a brief recap of the private conversation he'd had with his young assistant.

"He'll live high on that for quite some time with the other kids," was Hugh's comment. "And once everyone else has heard the story—I imagine it will be halfways round the village already!—you'll no doubt find you've not done your own reputation any harm either. We don't change too quickly in these parts. We respect old habits, traditional ways of doing things. The idea of *a MacDairmada* wanting to return to the village, even for a short time, taking an interest in the history of the village and the people who live here, and making a special effort to be approachable, even by the youngsters, it all counts for something, you know! Oh, yes, indeed."

Sure enough, as the pub gradually filled up, Phil was aware of people coming over to greet him, introduce themselves, or offer further information that they thought might be of some relevance to his supposed research into his family history. He felt a little uneasy with this, as it was to some extent a deception on his part, but once he started jotting things down, he realized that this was a perfect opportunity to go as deep as he could with his family tree project. He had been working on it in fits and starts for a couple of years, but had never really had the time to organize himself properly.

Kate was able to assist with the recording of tales and anecdotes. She'd served her time as a shorthand secretary, and managed to take detailed notes throughout the evening. The stories continued to flow in and she was obliged to call a brief halt at one point while she escaped to the caravan for a Dictaphone and a box of cassettes. By the time Michael Ashe decided to call time, Phil estimated they had at least a fortnight's editing and cross-referencing ahead of them.

"Most of the stories seem to have a lot in common; the same details keep coming up again and again. Christ, I sound like a bloody cop looking for evidence," he muttered as they sat over a final coffee before turning in. He stretched and yawned.

"What's that line from Gilbert and Sullivan? 'Corroborative detail, intended to give...?'" said Kate.

"'To give artistic verisimilitude to an otherwise bald and unconvincing narrative.'" Phil completed the famous excuse offered by Lord-High-Everything-Else Pooh-Bah for his prevarications in the plot of *The Mikado,* and grinned at the thought. "I just hope there's a more solid foundation in fact with this tale, otherwise we're wasting our time."

"You don't really think that, though, do you, Phil?"

"No, definitely not! There's far too much detail, which different people have offered, totally independent of each other. This tale covers who knows how many generations, and it dovetails so neatly with what I can remember of what I read on the 'Net. There may well be some embellishments and adornments here and there that have been added through the years by the oral tradition of telling and retelling the story, but in essence, it's family history rather than imaginative fiction. I believe it's based on solid historical fact. At least, the names and dates are checkable. They seem to be right from what I can remember... It's late, and quite honestly, I'm too shattered to log on and run it past the website."

"How shattered *are* you then, Phil?" she purred.

"Never *that* shattered, sweetheart. Want me to prove it?"

Chapter Five

When Phil woke the following morning, he felt as if he'd had the best night's sleep in years. For what seemed the first time in living memory, it wasn't a strident alarm clock's imperative nag that roused him. It was a heartbeat or two before he identified the sound of a persistent, gentle rain pattering on the roof of the caravan. The vehicle's hollow timber frame magnified the sound and mellowed it, reminding him of the compulsive, rhythmic tattoo of the *bodhrán* drum, which had woven skilfully through so many of the traditional songs he'd enjoyed listening to the previous evening.

He sensed that it was still quite early in the day. He fine-tuned his townie ears to identify other sounds behind the silvery, almost melodic tinkle of the light rain. A bird of some sort called a greeting, answered immediately by a near-identical, fainter response—presumably a partner some distance away? The caravan had been parked in the lee of a row of chestnut trees; the wind soughed through the leaves overhead, teasing the brass ornaments on the roof eaves into a brief jangle of merriment as it passed. There was no hint of the angry snarl of early morning commuter traffic. A low-lying early morning mist on the grass replaced the noxious exhaust fumes of city living, and the low, pale sun clearing a stand of trees was a far more welcome sight than the harsh neon streetlamp that he suddenly—and irrationally—decided he hated for daring to intrude on the privacy of his bedroom.

First things first. Kate was still sprawled on her side of

the bed, and he knew that she loved to be awakened with the seductive aroma of the day's first brew of coffee tantalizing her nostrils. Kettle on, coffee measured into the percolator...

With a stab of guilt, he upbraided himself. Perhaps he should have thought of grooming Gerald before seeing to his and Kate's own personal needs? He pushed open the half-doors at the front of the caravan and discovered that he was too late. Sean had already led Gerald into the stable and was almost finished grooming.

"Sean, do you never sleep?"

Sean had been running back and forth in his capacity as pot-boy throughout the evening's session in the pub, and Phil was pretty sure that he would have been washing glasses and tankards for some time after the last guests had left.

Sean grinned and automatically glanced at the sun as he replied, "Sure, an' God's good light's been on the land an hour and more. Why wouldn't I be up and about my chores?"

This could have sounded po-faced or insincere, but under the circumstances, and coming from Sean , somehow, it didn't. He had a natural, unforced, and innocent charm about him that appealed to Phil, who grinned in turn as he clambered off the steps of the caravan and stretched out a hand. "At the least you can allow me to help you finish off the job, or old Gerald will start to forget who's paying for his meals! Can you run over and ask Michael what time he wants to serve breakfast?"

Sean looked to the skies and nodded. "My pleasure, Uncle Phil, though I'm thinking it's not looking like it's going to stop raining any time soon, so breakfast is likely to be a leisurely affair today!"

Phil agreed with the young lad's assessment of the weather.

"This must be what my gran used to call 'Ma Reilly's Washing Day,'" he responded. Sean's features creased in amusement. Kate, appearing sleepily at Phil's shoulder, hadn't heard the full exchange. Putting her arms around him, she nibbled gently at his earlobe and fixed him with a stare that demanded an explanation.

"My mam's ma, Grannie Ellen, used to say that the only thing this weather was good for was to get the washing done!" he said with a self-conscious grin.

"All the same" he continued, "it gives us an excuse to sit down and sift through all the notes we've got to date; just reading the notes we took in the bar last night will probably take the best part of the day."

Sean was clearly heartbroken. "Will you not be wanting to row out to the island and take more photies?"

Phil shook his head gently. "I'm pretty certain we'd not get anything useful in this weather; the light's poor, and we need clear, detailed pictures," he explained. "And one of the things I'd like to get done today might seem a bit of a boring job, but I really need your help. I need to catalogue all the prints, sort them out by where they were taken from, what time of day they were taken, which part of the building we're looking at...believe me, Sean , there's a lot of detective work to do, and I just *know* you'd be good at it!"

His ego massaged, Sean puffed his chest out and ran off to order breakfast from Michael Ashe, who appeared as if telepathically summoned a split-second before the pot-boy's headlong dash seemed destined to rip the kitchen door from its hinges.

"Would our house guests be breaking their fast now?" he asked as Sean skidded to a seemingly impossible stop centimeters from a full-frontal collision. Phil raised his mug to conceal a grin and nodded his confirmation. Michael raised his hand in acknowledgement and turned to re-enter the kitchen.

Kate had disappeared to dress, and returned before Phil emptied his mug. "Come on, this isn't fair. You're a cup ahead of me already!" She pouted facetiously. Phil's response was to catch her around the waist and embrace her. The years they'd been together were of little or no consequence; Kate's bright smile and gentle laughter played havoc with his heartstrings and always would.

It was Kate who—reluctantly—broke off the tender morning greeting when she saw the kitchen door start to swing open. Sean crossed the courtyard at a more sedate pace than he'd demonstrated a few minutes earlier and escorted them back to the main bar. He left them briefly, and they heard the sound of running water beyond a half-closed door before he reappeared with slicked hair, washed hands, and an old-fashioned butler's apron tied around his waist, ready to wait on for the "house guests."

Once he had ensured that they both had what Michael called "a sufficiency" on their plates, he waited for a nod of permission from the proprietor before serving himself an equally impressive portion, which disappeared rapidly.

The resultant empty plates, cutlery, and serving dishes vanished just as quickly and efficiently as the meal. Phil was barely aware of Sean's presence as he flitted back and forth, but as he poured himself a third cup of coffee, he was suddenly aware of the fact that the table was completely empty. Sean hovered patiently with a damp cloth in his hand, ready to wipe down surfaces.

"If you've anything you might need from the caravan, I can clean up in here for you. There's much more room for you to work on these tables than there is in the caravan."

Kate settled at a round table against one wall with half a dozen notebooks, a box full of audio cassettes, and a tape recorder. Phil had taken the washing up bowl from the caravan's miniscule kitchen and filled it with envelopes, each stuffed with photographs. Sean drifted between the two, dancing with suppressed excitement, but settled at Phil's elbow as soon as he sat down and fanned out the envelopes like a stage magician with an oversized deck of playing cards.

"The first thing you can do for me, Sean, is to sort them all by the time they were taken. The time's printed here, in the top right corner, okay? Then we can go through them together and try to break them down into other sets, like what building they show, or from what angle..."

Phil had no reservations about treating Sean as an adult, an employee. What the youngster lacked in experience was more than compensated for by his enthusiasm. Phil also saw something of himself in Sean. He'd known, at more or less the age he estimated Sean to be, that he wanted to carve a professional career in photography. Before long, Sean proved that Phil's confidence wasn't misplaced. He had a good eye for detail, and the fact that every photograph was in the sharp, crisp contrast of black and white made this extremely valuable.

Of course, they were without exception night shots and had been taken without the benefit of a flash gun, but the clarity of each print was excellent. Sean soon had them sorted in a dozen or so piles of varying heights, but there three

three or four that brought a frown to his young face. He laid these on one side and studied them carefully for a few minutes before passing them over to Phil for a second opinion.

"I can't work out if these are smudges of some sort," he said, pushing the prints across the table. The prints, four in all, were centered on the main door of the chapel. The blemishes were in the foreground, as if someone or something had crossed rapidly in front of the lens at the exact moment the shutter had been released. The shots were from three different camera angles. Three of them were timed between 01:30:30 and 01:30:50. The odd one out was from one of the same three cameras, judging by the angle, and timed ten minutes later at 01:40:30.

"It has to be close to the ground, and angled upwards," Phil murmured. "It might be a bit distorted, for that reason, but there doesn't seem much doubt about it. As far as I can tell, we're looking at an image of a person—the low angle makes it hard to decide on their height. I get the impression the figure's female. But nobody spent the night on the island, and if they had, they'd surely have been missed in the pub!"

Kate had abandoned her notes and cassettes and was leaning over Phil's shoulder. Michael Ashe was close by, one step further to Phil's left.

"What say you, Michael? Are we all imagining things?"

Michael shook his head gravely. "I think it's time to send word for Hugh O'Gara. The *seanch'ai*'s the only person I can think of who might be able to shed some light on this…"

Chapter Six

The Eldest Resident's name had barely passed Michael Ashe's lips when the door opened, framing Hugh O'Gara in a backlight of brilliant sunshine. The early morning squalls of rain had been banished from that particular corner of Roscommon, at least temporarily

"*Siochan teach!* Peace to the house!" Hugh raised his right hand in token of greeting as he spoke. He headed for his customary armchair, at one side of the open fireplace. Michael was there ahead of him with a small glass in his hand, and helped him off with his cloak.

"It can't be just chance, or coincidence," Kate said. "But how could he possibly *know*...?"

Hugh looked up and caught her eye.

"Maybe you shouldn't be shouting so loud f'r assistance, young lady! Sure, I could hear you as soon as I passed the Post Office! Now, how can I help?"

Phil came to her rescue. "Michael just suggested that you were the best person to ask about something we...well, we're not sure exactly what it is. We were looking at some photographs, timed shots from the cameras we set up last night on Castle Island."

Sean was there at once with the four prints in question. Hugh thanked him gravely, nodding when the young lad drew his attention to the times printed in the upper corners. He studied each of them carefully, giving most of his attention to the "odd one out." A feeling of peace settled on the room, a comfortable, meditative silence with no hint of threat or tension.

When Hugh looked up again, his pale blue eyes were calm, serene. For some reason, Phil immediately felt an overwhelming sense of relief.

"Do you see what I *think* I see in that last frame?" he asked.

"Some sort of figure, you mean? Not solid, nor with a defined shape, more *taibhse*, not of this world...perhaps a *meabhair*, a memory of some earlier time would be more accurate than ghost or spirit. Is that what you see?"

"To me it seemed a female figure of some sort," Phil replied. "And Michael felt that if there was anything in history that might explain it, you'd be the one to ask."

"History's being made every day, all around us, and what little I've observed in my lifetime is only a few poor sentences at the end of a long tale told to me by my grandfather before he passed on, and that concluding with his own few thoughts tacked on to what he learnt at his grandfather's knee, and so on back in time. I had th' advantage of knowing my letters, but he had no book learning, yet he was without doubt the wisest man I knew. The tales he told me are old, older than the hills, even before the time the Blessed Padraig brought news of the New Religion to Tara and Moylurg.

"Castle Island, or McDermot's Rock, has been in the family's hands since they wrought the Kingdom of Tara and the Seat of Moylurg from the O'Conor clan, who were high kings before them. The castle followed with the land and the title, and was the seat of power for many generations. The Seven Kingdoms gradually melded to form a single country with an elected government rather than a small number of powerful families contesting to rule as far as they could reach. Tara was the largest of the Seven Kingdoms, and the last to concede.

"There has been no maintenance of the grounds now for many generations, and the island has become overgrown, but it's all superficial, and could, with a determined effort, be sculpted and restored at least in part to reflect some of its former glory. Much of the island is, in fact, very rocky, with only a thin veneer of soil and a scant covering of grass.

"In its best years, it was rich in game and sport, but could never support the growing of crops. The MacDermot was always obliged to buy in grain, vegetables, and other food, which rankled with many of the chieftains through the years.

"But the third name, now, Trinity Isle." Hugh paused a moment and closed his eyes, as if turning a page in an internal tome of memories and reminding himself of what his grandfather had recounted to him as a nervous young postulant to the role of the *seanch'ai*.

"The story is that early in his travels, before he had spread the Christian message throughout the Seven Kingdoms, the Blessed Patrick visited Moylurg and was a guest for several nights with the high king at that time, Donal O'Conor.

"It was during this visit Patrick first noticed the shamrock's form, and had the idea of using its unique triskele shape to describe the three-in-one nature of God to unlettered folk. This is the explanation I was given when I asked a similar question to the one you asked me regarding why this small island is honored with three different names, and until someone can offer me a more plausible reason for the name Trinity Isle, I'm quite happy to accept it as true!"

"And this 'memory' from last night's photograph, surely it can't refer to an incident *that* far back in time?" Phil queried.

Hugh shook his head at once. "No, no! This memory, this *meabhair*, must have some connection with the history of the island, and the clan, but as to a more precise time period, there's only one episode in the clan's history in which a female member of the family is a prominent figure."

Phil looked at the image on the photograph again with this in mind. Suddenly, he realized that the loose, flowing gown billowing around the neck and shoulders of the female figure was not, in fact, clothing, but long, pure white, untameable cascades of hair.

"Una Bhan?" he gasped in disbelief. "But, Hugh! You told us that the story of Una Bhan and Tomàs Laidír was from, what? Four hundred years ago? A legend, you said! Are you now suggesting it might be an actual, historical fact?"

Hugh shrugged, apparently unperturbed. "There are many stranger things I've seen, heard, experienced in my lifetime, Phil! It's not for me to try and decide where the line must be drawn between history and legend, but I've a suggestion you might wish to consider."

"Michael told us you were the best person to ask for advice."

"Well, the day's dried out and it's still early afternoon. Why don't you take yourselves off and have a look over the island in daylight hours? Photographs are all well and good, but you won't get the same 'feel' from them as you'll have from the sounds and even the smells of the island itself. Young Sean can stop hiding in the kitchen and pack you a picnic hamper. I'm sure he'll offer to row you out there and carry messages back if you need anything!"

"We'd both prefer it if you'd care to join us, Hugh, and grant us the benefit of your knowledge of the island and the general history of the region," Kate said. "I really want to find out as much as I can about the area while we're here."

Although it was no more than a gentle three hundred meters down a modest slope to the lough, Sean was despatched to the stables to harness Gerald to the caravan for Hugh's convenience. There was also plenty of space for some cold drinks and a selection of Kate's artist materials.

Sean led them onto a miniscule jetty at the southernmost point of the lough and handed Kate into the stern seat with a gravity of purpose far beyond his years. Hugh took the short seat in the prow, and Sean took care to balance the cargo evenly once Phil had settled next to Kate.

"Stable groom, part-time waiter, and now expert sailor, is there no end to your talents, Sean?" Phil murmured as their self-appointed ferryman plied the oars and skimmed effortlessly across the placid surface of the lake. Sean grinned and shrugged his shoulders, clearly too embarrassed to reply. Kate trailed her fingers in the water; it was warmer than she'd expected it to be. There was a suggestion of a heat haze at the far end of the lough, and the faintest possible breeze carried with it a potpourri of wildflower scents.

Hugh smiled at her. "Wade in slowly, if you're ever minded to take a swim! It gets very cold very quickly not far below the surface!"

Leaving Sean with instructions to collect a picnic lunch from the pub, Phil and Kate strolled across the narrow cove at a pace they sensed was comfortable for Hugh, heading for the remains of the chapel.

As soon as they stepped under the trees, Phil felt the difference in temperature, though it couldn't have been more than two or three degrees cooler. More difficult to explain was the sudden absence of all extraneous sound, as if they had suddenly been cocooned in their own little world, a private, exclusive mini-environment. There was neither bird song nor sigh of breeze to be heard, and a curious lambent quality to the light added a final touch to the feeling of utter peace and security that settled on the group. Kate chose a convenient rock to sit on and pulled out a pad. With eyes half-closed, she began to sketch; the outline of the chapel ruins grew swiftly under her dancing fingers.

Phil stood at Kate's shoulder, watching her settle to her work. As always, he marveled at her—to his mind—uncanny ability to conjure images almost as detailed as his best photo shots with a few simple tools. She was absorbed in the project and seemed unaware of her audience. After a few moments, he nodded to Hugh and offered his arm for support. Hugh shook his head politely.

"The ground's not that uneven, and as long as I have my *siúil* at my side, I'll manage to get by!" he said, flourishing the ancient, weather-beaten walking stick he carried everywhere. They left Kate and wandered closer to the main door of the chapel. Phil drew the "odd man out" photograph from his pocket and altered their path slightly to approach the building from the trajectory shown by the camera angle. He glanced down when he judged them to be in approximately the right place, and saw the static camera by his ankles. Hugh noticed the camera too, and turned to approach the remnants of the chapel entrance.

The remaining walls around three sides of the chapel were of dressed stone, which despite the ravages of nature in the time that had passed since the building was last used for its intended purpose, still appeared reasonably sound. The fourth wall, the one where the main entrance would have been, was somewhat the worse for wear, but there were still some stones that had not crumbled away entirely. As he stepped within the walls, Phil was immediately aware of a high-pitched whine inside his skull, the one that demands absolute, total silence all around before the listener is aware of it. The last few faint sounds of nature ceased. His own shallow, effortless breathing was the only thing he could hear.

The flagged floor of the chapel seemed almost entirely free of any grass and weeds, which struck him as odd considering there had been no attempt at maintaining the building in who knew how many years since it had been in use. Perhaps a tribute to the quality of its construction, he told himself, though he doubted this to be the whole truth. The silent, peaceful scene was truly timeless, untouched.

Hugh stirred at his side, and advanced on the one remaining structure within the walls, a stone table at the far end, which Phil knew had to be the altar stone. He followed the *seanch'ai*, a respectful pace or two behind him. As they reached the altar, Hugh closed his eyes, bent his head, and crossed himself. Automatically, Phil followed suit and tried to clear his mind of all the thoughts and questions that welled within his head. After a few seconds, Hugh raised his head and regarded Phil thoughtfully.

"There's an ancient power in this place, and I sense you're aware of it!"

There was something in the older man's tone of voice that Phil wasn't expecting. Somehow, it suggested the respect of a young person for an older member of the family, or the deference of a loyal worker petitioning a loved and trusted boss for a favor. Phil felt slightly uneasy; as a child he'd always been told that he should always honor and respect older people he met. To him, this sudden reversal of roles felt quite simply wrong.

"I can certainly feel there is a wonderful peace on this island," he heard himself say. It was almost as if someone else was speaking through him. He had no clear idea of what he was going to say next until the words came tumbling from his mouth, seemingly of their own accord without any conscious mental effort on his part. "It feels as if we could be here at any time, any day in the three hundred years or more since my ancestors lived here. There's a timeless quality about the place."

"Ah! I'm glad I don't have to try and explain *that* to you, young man! Because if you hadn't sensed it for yourself, I'd be thinking you weren't yet ready..."

"Ready?"

"All in good time, Phil, all in good time! You asked me to come with you today as a guide, and to acquaint you with some more details of the McDermott Clan history. I'll be happy to oblige, but I'd like to know a few more things about you as well, if you don't mind?"

"Hugh, I'm grateful for what you've already taught me! Just ask, I'll gladly tell you anything I can about the family research I managed to complete before we turned up unannounced."

"So let me start by asking, are you an only or eldest child?"

Phil hadn't expected this line of questioning. In truth, he'd no idea where this might be leading, but at least it was an easy question for starters.

"I've two sisters, both younger than me."

Before he could ask the "Why?" question already forming on his lips, Hugh pressed on. "Almost as important, do you have any male cousins *older* than yourself? I have to ask because we need to trace where the clan has spread itself over the years."

Phil nodded. He could see the logic of this, even if he couldn't yet guess where Hugh might be heading, but he was still at ease, confident. This was still familiar territory, basic family research he had long since committed to memory. "My grandfather, Tomàs, was the oldest of seven brothers. They all left Roscommon to seek work; two of them managed to find passage to America and married there. Neither of them had children. Of the five who didn't go to America, Tomàs married first and had one son—my father—and four daughters. Two never married, and I eventually traced the remaining two. They both married later in life; one settled in Scotland, the other moved to London. Their children were several years younger than my father. Do you need more? I'd have to look at my notes for names and dates of birth..."

"That won't be necessary, at least not just now," Hugh murmured, pulling a pipe out of his pocket and catching Phil's eye with a tacit request for permission to smoke.

"So Tomàs was one of seven sons; yes, indeed, I'd forgotten that detail." He lit his pipe and ensured it was burning evenly "As it's inconceivable there could have been two Tomàs McDermotts, each from a family of seven sons *and* in the same generation, I think it's without question, you're of direct line. Now, Phil, since you're the first born male of *your* generation, I have to ask, are you prepared to accept the role of *an MacDairmada*?"

Chapter Seven

Phil stared, speechless. He hadn't been expecting Hugh's first couple of questions, but at least he'd studied enough of the clan history to be able to give some sensible answers. This question completely took the wind from his sails.

Hugh stood calmly and waited for an answer. Phil realized that he had no options; he had to say something.

"Hugh, assuming it can be proved that I'm of direct line, I need to know what's involved, what would be expected of me. What *is* the role you speak of?"

"That's a sensible approach, and no less than I'd expected of you!" Hugh chuckled.

"It's not as if there's any worldly goods to be had, or family jewels to inherit," he continued, "but for what it's worth, the MacDermot, or *an MacDairmada* if you will, may call himself Prince of Coolavin. Far more important is the fact that others will look to you as an example, someone who lives in a way fitting to the motto on the family shield. *Honor probatque Virtus*,—Honour and approved Virtue."

"And you're telling me that people would take it seriously if I were to 'lay claim' to the title. That's what you're saying," Phil declared, soberly and without even a hint of question or doubt in his mind that Hugh had meant every word literally. "That's a very real responsibility. You mean, people might some along asking my opinion about something or other, even help settle a dispute, like some kindly old Lord of the Manor?" To Phil, it all seemed unreal, even faintly ridiculous, but to his surprise, Hugh looked up and nodded sincerely.

"What you have to remember is, we aren't living in a big city where nobody really knows his neighbor. This is a quiet, settled, relatively small local community. We've two churches, two pubs, a local shop and the local GAA Club; the rest's all farming land, and not much has changed in several generations. Even the local *garda* lives in the next village, six miles away on his pushbike, but there's precious little crime, even so! And if someone were to accept the title of *an Mac-Dairmada*, I'm sure 'twould please everyone!"

"This is something I could never have dreamt of, something that is obviously going to affect many others! And how about Kate? How would all this affect her?" he demanded. "Apart from anything else, we've always made every major decision together. I couldn't just make a decision for us both without consulting her. She has a right to know!"

"Yes, Phil, I agree! Let's not be hasty, now!" Phil had been on the point of striding off to wherever Kate was to be found with her sketchpad until Hugh laid a restraining hand on his arm. "She won't be far away. In fact, I'd say she's more than enough scenery to paint and draw, she's not likely to have moved off anywhere! Your concern for her is yet another thing that tells me you would be a good role model for anyone! But there's just the one thing I've noticed, or, rather, *haven't* noticed..."

Suddenly, Hugh seemed almost embarrassed, as if he hesitated to broach a sensitive topic of conversation.

"I mentioned others looking to you for guidance. I couldn't help but notice, but although you both wear a ring, they don't 'feel' like wedding bands to me. Am I right?"

Phil was stunned. How on *earth* could Hugh have guessed...?

"Yet you sign the same family name in Michael Ashe's guest book," he continued, unperturbed. "You *are* married, I take it? No offense intended!" he added swiftly. For a split second, Phil thought the elderly *seanch'ai* blushed as he rushed the last words of his question. Belatedly, he realized why Hugh had been dancing all around the subject without posing the important question.

"Yes, Hugh, of course we're married! Almost four years now, but we've been together for over seven years."

"And I'm guessing it was a civic service, not in a church."

"That's right. We were newly-qualified students at the

time and poor as the proverbial church mice," he admitted. He was being completely honest, but even as he spoke, he felt as if he was hearing a feeble excuse rather than an explanation. Hugh nodded, but didn't comment.

"We need to find Kate. This is something you really *do* need to discuss with her as well!"

Kate wasn't very far away. She'd finished her sketching on the east bank of the island and moved around with the sun to the south flank, opposite the main entrance. Phil ran to greet her with a kiss.

"Don't unpack your gear just yet, darling. The sketches can wait! There's something we need to discuss with Hugh first, and perhaps we should raid the picnic boxes, at least for something to drink? I'm parched!"

◉ ◉ ◉

"Now don't get me wrong, I may be an old man set in my ways, but I hope I'm not a fool who tries to judge others."

Phil and Kate sat unconsciously hand in hand and told Hugh the few details that seemed necessary about their marriage in front of a few friends and family at the registry office in Liverpool.

"Of course, people get married in civil offices here in Ireland just as in every other part of the world. But the church is still central to our lives, especially in small, close-knit communities such as ours. Perhaps we live in a more traditional manner, not at the same mad pace as the rest of the world.

"No matter! You had good grounds for the decision you made at the time, and it's quite evident it works for you. But what if the next young couple in Kilronan who decide to spend the rest of their lives together come to the new *an MacDairmada* and his wife for advice? Suppose they, like you, hadn't decided on a church or registry office affair? Could you help them decide? And yes, if you decide you're prepared to accept the role of Clan Chief, it's very possible this is the sort of situation that might very easily present itself!"

"Hugh, after what you told us last night of Tomàs and Una Bhàn and their...what did you call it? Their hand-fasting? Even though they never married..." Kate hesitated. She seemed to be thinking carefully, picking her words with care. "That was also a way of declaring their devotion, their commitment to one another and nobody else, am I right?" Hugh nodded, and Kate carried on. "Phil and I talked about this last night when we were on our own..."

She glanced at Phil. He nodded, and picked up the thread. "We'd be obliged if you have any advice for us on the best way forward. What can't be changed, Hugh, is the fact that we were officially married three, almost four, years ago. That's on record in Somerset House or wherever the records are kept these days. That can't be altered, whatever position the Church takes on the subject!"

"Aye, true enough!" was Hugh's comment. He settled himself more comfortably on his tree stump.

"We decided that, if it means as much to your village community as you say, we'd like to find a way of..." He hesitated, unsure of how to express what he and Kate had discussed long into the night.

Kate stepped in. "What Phil's trying to say, Hugh, is can you perhaps ask Father Tomàs on our behalf for a blessing or something? Could you do that without causing too much gossip?"

Hugh sat and thought about this in silence for several long-drawn seconds. He seemed distant, lost in his private thoughts. The smooth meshing of Phil's and Kate's thoughts, the way they almost spoke as one, hadn't escaped his attention. He also thoroughly approved of the speed and decisiveness shown by the young pretender to the title of Clan Chieftain. The plan needed one final detail. This would be his personal contribution.

"Kate's idea of asking Father Tomàs for a blessing is a sensible one, and one that I believe has much to commend it. There are a number of couples I can think of who'd benefit from it, just as much as your good selves! At least you already have a pair of rings. Can I be so bold as to ask if your holiday funds would stretch to having some 'cosmetic work' carried out?"

"That won't be a problem!" Phil chuckled. He squeezed Kate's hand and continued. "We're both earning good money, and this is precisely when my 'flexible friend' earns his keep!" On an impulse, he turned to face Kate and dropped to one knee.

"This wasn't planned, sweetheart, but I never actually asked you at the time. It's about four years too late to ask you to marry me, but will you now do me the honor of wearing a genuine, blessed-and-full-working-order wedding ring?"

Tears sprang to Kate's eyes, tears of joy, as she immediately embraced him. "Of course I will, you idiot!" she spluttered

Phil tried, not too seriously, to shrug it off, and used the opportunity to steal another kiss as the surest way of silencing Kate's protests.

"So can I take that as a yes?" Hugh asked. He felt curiously privileged as a witness to this intensely personal commitment scene, rather than feeling like an uninvited interloper.

"You certainly can!" Phil replied. "I've been wanting to do something like this for ages. And it wouldn't surprise me to learn that you know someone, somewhere who can modify the rings?"

Hugh nodded thoughtfully, then stood and stretched himself. "We should head back to the shoreline; young Sean will be back soon with our lunch! I'll telephone my jeweler colleague when we get back, and I'll cycle over to speak to Father Tomàs this evening. Some things are better tackled face to face."

Chapter Eight

Sean arrived punctually with a picnic feast of impressive proportions, then fussed to set places for them all around a crisply laundered check tablecloth. A six-pack of Guinness and two red lemonades were left in the shallow water next to the rowboat to keep cool.

When the remnants of the meal had been packed together, Sean helped Hugh into the boat and paused before sitting on the thwart. "Will you be needing anything later on, Mr. Mc...Uncle Phil? Sandwiches, or a thermos of something warm to see you through the night?"

"That would be nice, Sean!" Kate cut in to spare Phil's blushes as she realized that he was berating himself for not having thought of such a simple thing himself.

"If you row across just about nightfall, that gives me time to potter about and set a few more cameras just the way I want them," Phil said.

Sean nodded gravely, giving the impression that this was the approving nod of a "fellow professional" photographer.

"Hugh might want you to help him pass an important announcement around the village," was Phil's parting shot. Sean's eyes grew round as millstones, and he all but caught a crab with a mistimed pull on the oars. A nod between Phil and Hugh indicated that the latter could begin to instruct Sean about Phil's attempt to overtrump the marriage feast at Cana with an open invitation to a party for everyone in the village to enjoy.

"That'll be all round the village before nightfall," commented Kate from behind Phil. She placed her hands on his shoulders, watching Sean's animated features as he spoke rapidly and excitedly to his passenger.

"I hadn't planned it this way, but perhaps it's better in a way that we're not staying in the village tonight as the news gets passed around," said Phil.

"Speaking of which, I've found a nice, snug little hollow full of a thick layer of dry leaves where we can spread out our sleeping bags. It looks like it's going to stay warm and dry tonight. We won't need a tent or anything. Dead romantic, hey?" She dug him in the ribs to emphasize her point.

The copse Kate had literally stumbled across was ideal for a night al fresco. By the time Sean returned with the promised snacks and warm drinks, Phil had also placed a number of cameras in prominent positions where Sean could not fail to notice them.

"Hugh says to tell you he'll introduce you to Father Tomàs after Mass on Sunday!" were Sean's first words almost before the skiff was safely grounded. He was obviously bursting with excitement and curiosity about the message, but too well-mannered to ask why this was important.

"Tell him thank you very much," Phil replied, and found it difficult not to smile at Sean's chagrin. "What time is Mass? Would you like to ride with us in the caravan?"

Sean brightened immediately at the prospect. "Thanks, are you sure you don't mind? We usually cycle over to Ardcarne; it's not that far."

"So you can sling your cycle in the back, if you want. Then you won't have to wait for a ride back if we get talking to the priest, will you?"

Sean beamed immediately at Phil's suggestion and rowed happily back to the shore.

Phil breathed a sigh of relief as they were finally left with some privacy for the evening. Considering the relative isolation of the village in the depths of rural Roscommon, they had not had a great deal of time on their own so far. Far from the relaxing holiday they had planned to help Kate cope with her frequent nightmares, it seemed as if they were being drawn inevitably into a scenario not of their own making, one which might even force them to make a number of decisions. It wasn't just the Church blessing of their marriage that was in question. Their whole lifestyle, including employment prospects, even where and how they chose to live in the future seemed to be in a state of flux. Briefly, Phil wondered if he was really in charge of his own destiny at the moment.

"Kate, have you had any of those...nasty dreams these last few days?"

"Mm-mm! Not since we left home, anyway. I've slept like a log!"

"I can't help wondering if there's a connection. I know you're not as uptight as you were before we flew out, but that's what we wanted to happen! I mean, what's the point of a holiday if you can't relax, eat too much, get drunk..."

"Get laid," murmured Kate as she gently led Phil to the nest she had made with their sleeping bags in the leafy hollow. As full night fell, in the seclusion of their own private island, they gently and slowly peeled from each other the few layers of clothing that the warm summer weather had demanded they wear for decency's sake.

※ ※ ※

Clothed once more, with an additional light sweater against the cool of the night around them, they sipped from coffee laced with Jameson's finest. Phil sat on a tree stump; Kate lay content with her head in his lap. Above, unseen and unheard, an owl swooped by on silent wings.

The small noises of the night gradually stilled, one by one, as the various daytime animals and birds settled. The "night shift," by their very nature, were more stealthy in their movements, more difficult to identify.

Keeping to his holiday resolution not to be governed by his wristwatch, Phil was aware of the advent of midnight when the pre-set timers on the cameras he had set out began to click. In the velvet silence of the night, the mechanical whirrs and clicks seemed louder than he would have thought possible.

They had the effect of rousing him from a pleasant state of half-dreaming reverie, and he stirred, easing the muscles in his lower back and thighs. Kate had also been drifting, and roused herself to allow Phil to stand.

A full moon shone in a cloudless sky. Every detail of the chapel was clearly defined. The moon was ideally placed, directly opposite the entrance and the steps. If the mysterious events of the previous night were repeated, there was every chance of clear, unambiguous photographic evidence, but of what? Phil wondered as he sauntered to the edge of the clearing, being careful not to wander in front of any of the strategically placed cameras.

Kate rose and followed him, quietly slipping her hand into his. "Do you think we're likely to see anything?"

"I'm trying to keep an open mind," he said. "But I've a sense of peace I've not felt anywhere else in a long time."

A long, inevitable kiss followed. They were distracted by a volley of almost simultaneous shutters being released from different points around the glade. Phil frowned. He had set the cameras to trigger at fairly well-spaced intervals in the interests of economy of film. He looked over Kate's shoulder to see if there was a reason for this salvo. There was only one possible cause he could think of.

He laid his hand gently on Kate's shoulder and turned her round to witness the scene. A young couple, dressed in clothing of a bygone era, floated rather than walked down the steps from the chapel. At the bottom of the steps, they turned to face each other, joined hands, and knelt. They seemed unaware of their audience. They were neither solid nor transparent, but almost monochrome, silvery grey or shimmery blue.

From where they were standing, they could see a three-quarter view of the man's face. The girl had her back to them, and her face was completely hidden behind a cascade of long, pale hair. The man's lips were moving, but no sound could be heard. He paused, as if listening to a response, then leaned forward and kissed her. As their lips met, the images faded away. Five—perhaps ten—impossibly long seconds of total and utter silence followed. The *click-click* of two more photo shots seemed as loud as cannonfire.

Imitating the actions of the lovers, Phil and Kate turned to face each other and joined hands as the players of the scene they had just witnessed had done. In perfect unison, they both began the same sentence.

"Did you just see—"

They stopped speaking at the same instant and looked each other deep in the eye. Neither knew exactly how they had intended to finish the question. Kate's expression might have been one of surprise tinged with awe, possibly fear of something unknown, unexplained. Phil felt a variety of emotions struggling for supremacy, but for him, the most important concern was Kate's wellbeing.

"It was when all the cameras all suddenly fired off at once," Phil murmured into Kate's thick tresses. "I knew that the only thing that could possibly have triggered it was something moving."

"Tell me what you saw," she insisted, drawing slightly away from his protective arms so that she could focus better on him as she waited for his reply.

"Two people in what I can only describe as old-fashioned clothes," he began. "I'm no fashion expert, but even I could see that much."

"It seems we both saw the same thing," Kate agreed. "And the girl, all I could see was her long, fair hair. I don't suppose you could see any more than me. It must have been more or less the same angle."

"That's right."

"I can make a guess that the clothes are from a period of, I don't know, at least two hundred years ago, but his face, Phil! Did you see his face?"

Phil shook his head, mystified at Kate's agitation. She gripped his forearms fiercely.

"Phil, he was so sad!"

Gently, Phil eased his arms out of her tense grip and stroked her long, thick mane of hair once more in a soothing gesture.

"I saw his lips move, but I heard nothing. I was thinking of the girl's white-blonde hair, and the tale Hugh told of Tomàs and Una Bhan last night...if you recall, her name means just that."

Chapter Nine

Neither Phil nor Kate felt like sleeping during what remained of the short summer night. When Sean pulled over to pick them up, Phil had already removed the film from the cameras and they were ready to step into the skiff and push off at once.

"Did you have a good night?" Sean asked as he pulled across the lake.

"It was peaceful, and a lovely night to sleep under the stars," Kate answered, squeezing Phil's hand to make sure he took his cue from her words.

"It certainly was," he agreed. "But I'll be interested to see what's on this set of film, if anything," he added, mentally crossing fingers and toes in the hope that this would be enough to satisfy Sean's curiosity and forestall potentially awkward questions. The tactic seemed to work. Sean nodded, shipped oars, and hopped ashore to help Kate out of the boat.

"It's almost eight o'clock. Michael Ashe will have your breakfast ready, so we can leave to drive over to Ardcarne for Mass by nine or thereabouts."

"Have you had breakfast, then?"

"Yes, thanks, Uncle Phil! And I've put my bicycle in the caravan like you said. I can be grooming Gerald and get him into the traces while you're eating."

His boyish eagerness and thoughtfulness impressed Phil greatly, as did the automatic use of the honorary title, which had Hugh's provisional approval. He made a mental note to ask Hugh privately if there was a suitable way to thank Sean for all his hard work.

Michael Ashe had laid out some cereals, with fresh bread, toast, some cheese, and a selection of jams.

"Just something to break your fast before you go over for Mass," he said, though neither Phil nor Kate had thought to question what was on offer.

"If you're peckish when you return, I can put an early lunch up for you."

"Michael, you've other things to do. You've a pub to run!" Kate protested.

Michael blushed, muttered something about he'd see how they felt when they got back from Mass, and left them to eat.

Sean was waiting for them when they emerged from the pub. He held Gerald's lead rein in one hand and smiled as he saw them. Gerald gleamed from nose to tail, the result of a thorough grooming from Sean, who had apparently also found time to polish up the brass and leather of the harness.

"Do you ever sleep, Sean?" Kate asked, only half-teasing. She was beginning to feel slightly uncomfortable about the special treatment everyone seemed to assume they deserved.

Sean appeared to consider the question perfectly reasonable. "Sure, my grandpa always says, 'Sleep? You're a long time dead!' and if that's good enough for him, I'm sure it's good enough for me!" he said blithely, and turned to hold Gerald's head more securely.

"Would you like me to hand you up, Aunt Kate?" he offered.

"Thank you, Sean, but I'm sure I'll manage," she said, raising the hem of the single "posh Sunday frock" she'd packed for the holiday and stepping carefully from wheel trim to buckboard and eventually to the broad bench seat, where she was immediately joined by Sean. Phil completed the line-up.

"You're in the middle, Sean. Would you mind driving, since you know the way to the church?" said Phil.

This seemed to make the young boy's happiness complete. Apparently unable to trust himself to speak, he nodded and chirruped Gerald into motion.

As they clopped along the road toward Ardcarne, they passed people, family groups for the most part, who had evidently left before them to walk the two miles or so to the neighboring village for Mass. Sean nodded and waved to everyone they met, and received smiles and greetings in return.

A bell began ringing as they entered the village proper. Sean drew up at the church gates, holding Gerald steady as his passengers stepped down.

"From the bell, Mass will start in about ten minutes, I'm thinking, but Father Tomàs may well wait if he knows one or two regular parishioners are still on their way," he said. He hopped down and led Gerald over to an ancient-looking but serviceable drinking trough.

At the main door of the church, they were greeted warmly by Father Tomàs. The church was filling up quickly, so they excused themselves and made their way to a vacant pew, which still had room for Sean, who scurried in to join them.

The congregation rose as Father Tomàs entered. He had changed and was now dressed in a green chasuble and stole. Two servers preceded him, one bearing the missal, the other a thurifer. The incense was delicate, not overpowering. It had been some time since he had last attended a church service. Phil hoped he could remember all the appropriate places to stand and sit.

"In ainm an Athar agus an Mhic agus an spioraid Naoimh. Amen."

Caught slightly flat-footed by the unexpected greeting, Phil automatically made the sign of the cross as he saw everyone around him doing. Fervently, he hoped that the whole service would not be conducted in a language—Gaelic, he assumed—that he had no chance of following. Father Tomàs paused, and to Phil's relief, continued in English.

"Welcome, brothers and sisters, to our celebration of the Mass today, and a special welcome to all our guests, visiting relatives and holidaymakers! Now, to prepare ourselves, let us call to mind our sins, and after that, can I ask you to join in singing the Gloria, which will be led by the children of the school choir?"

As the readings and prayers followed, Phil found himself falling into the familiar habits, knowing where to stand and sit, and following the Mass easily enough from the service sheet he found beside him on the pew.

He was almost caught again after Father Tomàs' homily, which felt more like a chat with a favorite uncle, and the prayers for the congregation, read by a parishioner. He had realized that this normally ended with the well-known "Hail Mary," but once again, he was obliged to pray silently as the rest of the congregation began once again in Gaelic.

"Sé do Bheatha Mhuire, Tá lán do ghrásta..."

"Hail Mary, full of grace..."

When it was time for the Our Father, just before Communion was given out, he was more or less expecting Gaelic to be used, and contented himself with listening to and enjoying the beauty of the fluid vowels and liquid rhythms of the language.

As they did not attend church regularly, Phil and Kate had decided to remain seated when the rest of the congregation filed to the altar rail to receive Communion. Father Tomàs, however, had other ideas and paused after the last parishioner had left the altar rail, and nodded encouragingly when he caught Phil's eye. Before the moment became embarrassingly long, Phil squeezed Kate's hand and they both rose and went forward.

Instead of offering them the host, Father Tomàs laid one hand on each of them in turn and spoke once more the words of the Sign of the Cross. Phil suddenly remembered from his childhood that this blessing was used by priests for non-Catholics who, for whatever reason, usually funerals, attended RC services.

After the Notices and Final Blessing, Father Tomàs reminded the congregation that there was tea and coffee in the hall adjoining the church, and made a point of including "all our guests, especially those far from home."

With such a strong hint, it would have been impossible for anyone to decline the invitation. Phil and Kate trooped self-consciously into the hall, but were quickly made to feel as welcome as if they had lived in Ardcarne all their lives. It quickly became apparent that Hugh O'Gara had not lost time in informing people of the identity of the holidaymakers. If they had taken a tape recorder or notepad with them, they could have had a dozen anecdotes about the McDermott family, and three or four times as many suggestions for further research into background history.

"I'll be cycling home now. Me ma says I've to be back for lunch."

Automatically, Phil looked for the watch he wasn't wearing, caught himself, and grinned at Sean, who had materialized at his elbow. Glancing around, he became aware of the fact that a majority of the congregation had each washed their own cups and departed, leaving Phil, Kate, and Hugh, along with the priest's housekeeper and a few stragglers as the only people still in the hall chatting with Father Tomàs. Hugh gave his cup to an elderly lady and said something to her. She trotted over to deliver it to the housekeeper and continued out of the door. Placing his hand on the arm of the last straggler, Hugh spoke a few words and began walking toward the door as the conversation developed. Phil had to admit that Hugh was a skilful diplomat. Neither of the parishioners seemed to realize they'd been politely railroaded to leave Phil and Kate the opportunity for a private conversation with Father Tomàs.

"Hugh tells me you're here on holiday, and to dig a little into your family history."

Father Tomàs sat at the nearest table, indicating that he expected to be there for some time. Phil and Kate joined him. Hugh closed the door on the final parishioner and stumped over to the group.

"We've not been here long, a matter of a few days, but we've found out a lot already, and Hugh has been very helpful in many ways," Phil began. "For example, I doubt we'd have found out so quickly about the history of the family, and the duties, responsibilities..." He made vague, exasperated hand gestures, indicating that he was unsure of the proper words to use. Father Tomàs nodded encouragingly. Phil continued. "I believe that certain things are...expected of someone who wishes to claim the title *an MacDairmada*. At least, that's what I understood from what Hugh was telling us. One of these things is something that I believe is within your field of expertise, and Hugh thought we should ask for your advice.

"Kate and I were both born into Catholic families, but neither of us have been regular churchgoers for many years. When we married three years ago, we were both recently graduated students and poor as the proverbial! So we opted for a simple civil service rather than the expense of a church wedding."

"What's important in the eyes of God is this, are you both committed to each other?"

The instinctive tightening of the mutual handclasp caused by the priest's interruption did not go unremarked, neither did the glance that passed between Phil and Kate as they nodded their confirmation.

"As I said, Father, we're not regular churchgoers, but Hugh thinks that we should ask you if you can see a way to...to regularize our marriage in the eyes of the church. As far as I understand what Hugh's told us, as a McDermott, possibly with some claim to the title, according to Hugh, I've a duty, a responsibility if you like, to set an example for others. I know that we can't 'go through the motions' of a church ceremony, which wouldn't be valid anyway! Also, it would be a form of deception, which would seem to defeat the whole object of the exercise. We'd really appreciate your professional advice, Father!"

For a moment, Father Tomàs sat silent, head bowed. Looking up, he stretched for Phil's free hand, and Hugh's. Hugh completed the circle by taking Kate's free hand.

"We should pray for guidance," he said simply. "The Lord's Prayer is the most powerful one I know. I hope you'll excuse me for using the Gaelic, but if you follow at your own pace in English, I'm sure the Lord is enough of a linguist to understand us all!"

Hugh spoke the opening Gaelic words. "*Ár n-athair, atá ar neamh,*" along with Father Tomàs. Praying silently, Phil listened again to the fluid rhythms of the ancient language, and discovered that the natural pauses he used at the end of a phrase appeared to be mirrored exactly in the version Hugh and Tomàs used.

After a short pause at the end of the prayer, Father Tomàs released Phil's hand and Hugh's. Kate and Phil continued their normal, natural clinch of fingers.

"How long are you planning to remain in Ardcarne? Do you have job responsibilities back in England, or any other diary dates you have to meet?"

"No, we're both self-employed, and much of my work I can do over the 'Net anyway," said Phil.

"And as an artist, I think I've probably completed more sketches and ideas in the last few days than I'd be inspired to do in a month at home!" added Kate.

"So a telephone line's about all you'd be needing?" asked Hugh.

"Not even that, really, although it's always useful to be able to speak to people! By and large, I tend to e-mail my contacts, and as long as I can recharge my laptop from time to time, I can get by with that. Anyone who needs me urgently has my mobile number."

"And the same applies for me, too," added Kate.

Father Tomàs nodded again with a satisfied expression.

"So, next Sunday, I shall make the sanctity of marriage a subject in my homily after the gospel, and finish with a special blessing for all married couples," he said with a glint in his eye. "By that time, you'll have a chance to meet and talk to people, make some more new friends. You really seem a genuine couple to me. I'd like to think you'll be back amongst us again."

Kate suddenly stiffened. "Father, it may not be my place to say this, because Phil and I haven't even discussed it yet, but—"

It was Phil's turn to interrupt. "I think I know what Kate's going to say. I didn't say anything before because I didn't want her to think I was putting unfair pressure on her. But I've felt more and more attracted to the idea of moving here permanently, even though we've been here such a short time! There's a certain...I don't know, a certain magic, almost, a sense of somehow belonging..."

"You both wear a ring. Were they bought as a pair?"

Puzzled at this change of subject from the priest, Phil and Kate nodded dumbly.

Father Tomàs took a stole from his pocket. "Would you mind if I have a closer look? And is it okay with you if I lay my stole over your wrists?"

Still in silence, they offered their left hands, palm down on the table. Father Tomàs laid his stole across their hands as he studied the plain gold matching rings. He looked up.

"Now, it's not my place to advise you on how you spend your money, that's not the 'professional advice' you asked for, and which I've tried to give you. But you might like to take that lazy lump Gerald for some exercise before he eats all the sweet grass in the village! Trot him as far as Boyle, go to the jeweler there, Paddy Ratner, and ask him if he can find a pair of *claddagh* and mount them on the rings for you. You'll find he's an excellent goldsmith, and an honest man."

Vague memories of having heard the word before struck

Phil, but Kate was totally lost.

"The *claddagh* represents two hands clasped in friendship," explained Hugh, glad to be a part of the conversation. "It's become something of a tradition over the years for a *claddagh* symbol to be added to wedding rings; sometimes the rings are bought with the *claddagh* already upon them."

The suggestion appealed instantaneously to both of them, conveying at once both a sense of old-fashioned courtesy and romance and at the same time, being a tangible, physical cementing of their commitment to each other and to the prospect of acting as role models for others in a manner befitting *an MacDairmada* and his wife.

Hugh cleared his throat. "Now, there was also the other matter we mentioned, namely the idea of the *ceilidg,* which the community here missed out on three years ago on the occasion of the marriage of *an MacDairmada*…so, when should I be telling Sean to start going around and telling people to find their party finery?"

Phil grinned. "Why, Hugh, that's obvious! As soon as Father Tomàs has given the special blessing for all married couples next Sunday! How soon afterwards could it be arranged?"

Chapter Ten

Hugh took the seat in the caravan left vacant by Sean returning home on his bicycle.

"You made just the right impression on Father Tomàs, I'm thinking," he said. He took a pouch out of his pocket and held it up, seeking permission from Phil to smoke. A few minutes went by while he filled and lit a pipe that had seen many years of service.

"What about the *ceilidg* we discussed? Can it be arranged at such short notice? How many people?"

Hugh chuckled and waved Phil to silence with the stem of his pipe. "We're very much into providing our own entertainment here, away from the big towns," he said. "With young Sean already cycled home before we even left the church, I'll be surprised if he hasn't already started hinting to the village that something's in the air!"

"How many should we be catering for, though?" Kate put in. "I mean, we're not exactly flat broke, but at the same time…"

Hugh nodded. "The whole village and a lot of the farms round and about will be there, but with bigger events like this, everyone brings something or other with them. Michael Ashe will be pleased to supply all the drinks. It's good business for him, and as long as you stand a round of drinks, the first round, so to speak, as people arrive, that will be about what's expected. Talk to Michael about how much to put 'behind the bar' to cover that."

Michael Ashe had to be told, of course, the reason behind

Phil's inquiry about a tab for a round of drinks, but even without Hugh's assurances, Phil was confident that he could rely on the barman's discretion. A price was named, which Phil thought extremely reasonable, so much so that he hesitated before offering his hand on the deal. "You're sure that will cover it?" he asked.

Michael Ashe grinned. "Sure, and I'd have the bar open anyway, whatever night o' the week it might be! With all the food being brought in by guests themselves, it's actually less work for me. All I have to do is make sure the ovens are ticking over to keep certain dishes warm. I'll be looking to get some extra waiting on staff from outside the village, though, so I'll need to know as soon as you've settled a date!"

Sean, of course, was almost dying of curiosity and throughout the remainder of that typical sleepy rural Irish Sunday, tried a number of times to discover what the important announcement might be. It was all Phil could do to placate the boy without appearing brusque or outright rude.

"You'll have to wait a few days. There are things I need to do, people I need to speak to, before I say anymore," was all Phil could tell him, and with that, Sean had to be content.

Monday morning dawned bright and fresh, promising to be another unspoiled summer day. Deciding that it would be as good a way as any other of avoiding further interrogations from Sean , Kate and Phil groomed and harnessed Gerald while waiting for the day's first brew of coffee. They took the road to Boyle, intending to visit Paddy Ratner, jeweller, to inquire about the *claddagh* design for their rings, as suggested by Father Tomàs. Gerald seemed in good spirits after the couple of days' unaccustomed rest, but was impeccably well-behaved as he made light of the five miles to Boyle, southwest of the Lough.

Phil but turned on a transistor radio for a time check. The first station he found offered a pleasant mix of traditional Irish folk tunes and contemporary chart music, so after establishing that it was just after eight-thirty, he left it playing in the background.

Honeysuckle was blooming in the hedgerows on both sides of the road. As the sun rose over the treetops and the heat of the day began to make itself felt, the aroma of the blossoms spread and filled the air without becoming overpowering. The cries of far-off birds and the buzz of bees working in the flower-filled verges were the only sounds other than the muted radio. Too far away to be seen, a tractor throbbed a bass line to nature's melody. Other than that, they could have believed that they were the only people awake that glorious morning.

It was not quite nine o'clock as they clopped into Boyle. Belatedly, Phil wondered if there might be a problem parking the caravan. After all, this was Ireland, 2005, not Dodge City circa 1850, and one couldn't expect to find a "hitching rail" outside the Last Chance Saloon on Main Street.

He breathed a sigh of relief, therefore, when he saw the navy blue uniform of a member of the *garda* walking toward them, and asked if there was somewhere he might be allowed to tether the horse while they attended to some shopping. He was directed to a layby just away from the town centre.

"Just turn left at the next crossroads and you'll see it straight away. 'Tis only a short walk back, and the travelling people use it all the time, though I don't think there's anyone there today," the officer concluded, and stood at the side of the road until he saw them negotiate the corner before giving them a cheery wave and continuing on his beat.

Halfway along the slight widening of the road, which had to be the optimistically-named layby, was a five-barred gate. Twin ruts across the grassy verge suggested that it was used fairly frequently by wheeled vehicles. The track continued beyond the gate, which was not padlocked and swung easily on oiled hinges at a light touch. Perhaps thirty yards from the road, they pulled up under a stand of trees, which promised a fair degree of shade for most of the day, and close to a clear, pebble-bottomed stream. As soon as he was released from the shafts, Gerald headed straight to the water's edge and drank deeply, even before inspecting the lush grazing available.

Having made sure that Gerald was comfortable and that the gate was secure, Phil and Kate wandered hand in hand back toward the main crossroads of the town.

"Breakfast first, I think!" said Phil, scanning the shop fronts for a café or similar institution. Spotting one, he held the door open for Kate.

Two of the eight small round tables were occupied, and a smiling waitress held out a chair at a vacant table close to the front window.

"Would you like a morning paper while you wait for your meal, sir?"

Slightly surprised, Phil could only nod. Within seconds, the waitress returned with two different newspapers and a teapot of impressive dimensions.

"We'd like a full cooked breakfast, please," he said. A smile, a nod, two teacups, and two saucers materialized from nowhere, and the waitress withdrew once more. Phil looked dubiously at the teapot.

"I suppose it comes automatically with the meal," said Kate, reading his thoughts as clearly as if they were printed on his forehead.

Phil grinned and poured two cups. "Can't remember the last time I drank tea with a meal," he grunted. His face changed as soon as he sipped at it, and now it was Kate's turn to grin.

"Not as bad as you expected, then," she teased. There had been times in the past when Phil had opted for water rather than drink tea.

"Not bad," he conceded, and opened his newspaper to hide his embarrassment.

Their breakfast arrived swiftly, before he'd even managed to do more than glance at the headlines on the sports pages. It measured up in every respect to the generosity they had experienced at Michael Ashe's pub. A fresh pot of tea replaced the one they had been served while waiting for their order, and they indulged themselves with a leisurely meal in keeping with the distinctly slower tempo of life in Ireland. The Town Hall clock chimed ten as they finished the meal and Phil asked the waitress for the bill.

"Can you direct us to the jeweler's? Paddy Ratner, I was told to ask for," asked Phil as he paid at the till.

"Cross the square and look down to your left. Paddy's is near the zebra crossing. You'll see the beacons flashing." The cashier's glance dropped for a split second to check Kate's hands, and Phil could imagine her checking to see if they might be buying either an engagement ring or a wedding ring. He managed to keep a straight face as he added a generous tip to the total shown on the bill.

The window display at the jeweler's was discreet but tasteful. Some larger items, such as carriage clocks, were strategically placed to attract attention. More personal jewelery—rings, bracelets, and necklaces for example—were mounted on individual cards that could easily be removed for closer inspection by customers

An old-fashioned mechanical bell trilled as they pushed the door and entered. For a brief second, Phil felt slightly disoriented. It was almost as if they had stepped directly into a Dickensian emporium.

Two comfortable-looking armchairs were positioned on either side of a small occasional table in one corner. Above and behind this grouping, a display of coats of arms and other heraldic devices decorated the back wall of the shop.

"Good morning! How can I help you?"

Phil refocused his attention on the speaker, whom he assumed must be the proprietor.

"Mr. Ratner? I was advised to speak to you about a special piece of jewelery."

The jeweler had been polishing a tankard as they entered. Laying his cloth on the worktable behind the serving counter, he rose and offered a hand to his customers. "And may I ask who I have to thank for sending such a pleasant young couple my way?"

"Hugh O'Gara: he lives near Michael Ashe's Pub in Drumlion."

"And if Hugh O'Gara told you to ask after Paddy Ratner, then I'm honored to be of service! And you would be?"

"Phil and Kate McDermott, from Liverpool."

"Then I'm doubly honored to help in any way I can. *Cead Mile Failte!* A hundred thousand welcomes!" Paddy raised the hinged flap in the counter and came out to them, bringing with him the stool he had been sitting on and indicating they should sit in the corner chairs.

"Mr. Ratner, Hugh told us that you were the best person to ask about having a *claddagh* design added to our rings

The jeweler blinked, then took off his glasses and polished them scrupulously. From a waistcoat pocket, he produced a magnification lens and clipped it onto the frame. "Are the rings a tight fit, or can you take them off for me? I can examine them on your hands if you'd rather, but—ah, thanks!"

Phil had anticipated that this would probably be necessary, and they both removed their rings without difficulty.

Paddy examined them carefully, nodding his approval. "You've good quality gold here, and the rings themselves have been well looked after. There are no scratches or damage. I'm sure they'll take a *claddagh* without problems! Would you like a quotation, or are you ready to look at some designs?"

"Hugh told us what the *claddagh* looks like, so we're happy to be advised by you, sir."

"Sir, indeed! Paddy, please. In the circumstances, it's surely myself should be saying 'sir' to *an MacDairmada*, I'm thinking!"

Although he had had this reaction from a number of people already, Phil nonetheless felt a bit awkward about the effect the honorary title had. "I can't be certain the title's mine to claim," he protested, "and I don't look for any special treatment or favors, but for us, it's quite important to have the work done as quickly as possible. Ideally, before the week's out?"

"That won't be a problem; I've the metals and the tools to do it for you in good time. Would you care to tell me how you came to ask for this commission?"

Before he knew it, Phil found himself explaining to the jeweler the reasons for the addition of the *claddagh*, and the special blessing that Father Tomàs intended to convey on every married couple present at Mass in Ardcarne the following Sunday.

"And I know I've no right to ask this, Mr. Ratner, but I hope I can rely on your discretion, at least until after the event," Phil concluded.

"This isn't Father Tomàs' confessional box, but I can keep a confidence as well as anyone else! Now, all I really need to know is how large or how small you'd like the finished design to be. Then I can give you a fair idea of the price, depending on the amount of gold used and the time it takes."

By the time the details had been discussed and a time for trying on the rings agreed, the morning was well advanced. Phil insisted on paying the estimated cost up front, and in response, Paddy had declared that the sun had to be "above the yardarm" somewhere or other in the world, and poured three glasses of Jameson to seal the bargain. By the time they made their excuses and left, it was close to eleven o'clock and Kate was starting to worry about leaving Gerald unattended for so long.

"It's not as if we're going to find a parking ticket stuck to the caravan," joked Phil, but felt a bit concerned about leaving the horse, the caravan, and all their luggage. His worries were groundless, of course. Gerald was unquestionably glad to see them. Kate fussed over him and poured an extra helping of the special malted feed Patsy Slattery had provided, with strict instructions to make sure Gerald was given a generous helping at least once a day.

"We aren't in the back streets of Liverpool, you know," Kate scolded when Phil commented on the fact that nobody had attempted to steal anything in their absence.

"Amen to that!" was his response. They both laughed, and hitched up the wagon for the trip back to Drumlion and whatever Michael Ashe might be able to offer for lunch.

Chapter Eleven

Phil and Kate decided that the easiest way to avoid awkward situations in Drumlion—and having to deal with direct questions from Sean —would be to play the tourist for a day or two.

"When all's said and done, we're supposed to be on holiday," he said to Kate as they prepared to turn in on Monday evening. "Also, we don't want to deliver Gerald back to Patsy Slattery carrying a beer belly from lack of exercise!"

They had taken their route map to the pub and consulted Hugh on a number of possibilities. This had the added advantage of making it easier to steer casual conversation in directions they wanted it to flow and avoiding potentially difficult questions about their intentions and the important announcement, concerning which Sean had already dropped a number of none-too-subtle hints. They had opted to circumnavigate Loch Cé in a clockwise direction, stopping each night at a different campsite. From the list that Patsy Slattery had supplied, there seemed to be plenty to choose from. There appeared to be a pub or a farm every ten miles or so around the lake. Phil reckoned they could look forward to at least three days on their own, which would see them back in the village on Friday with less than two days to avoid Sean and his anxious questions.

They made a show of a deliberately casual start to Tuesday, lingering over breakfast. They stocked up in Kilronan's only shop with a modest amount of fresh food to carry with them, and eventually left late in the morning. Their first stop,

Clogher, was a village, which on the map looked to be of similar size, halfway along the west bank. The jungle drums, however, had preceded them, and at the pub when they stopped to ask about overnight parking, they were greeted with the *an MacDairmada* honorific.

"News carries quickly then," Phil said as he eventually managed to persuade Tommy McCardle, the innkeeper, to accept payment for their drinks.

"Sure, there's not much we don't hear about just as soon as it happens here. It's a quiet life in the country, and people are more interesting topics of conversation than crops or the weather. But you've been here a week now, you must have noticed that yourself!"

"Hugh O'Gara did say that he was going to be talking to some people about...about arrangements for a special day next week, but I wasn't sure how far he'd be spreading the news."

"Sure, and he asked me to let him have my two girls who usually serve at weekends. I gather there's to be a *ceilidg* next weekend?"

"I don't know the details yet, but that's right," admitted Phil. "But it's supposed to be a surprise, so if you can try to keep it that way, I'm sure Hugh would appreciate it!"

"If Hugh's been doing the rounds to get people cooking, you can be sure that people will be well aware there's a *ceilidg* in the offing! Still, there'll be good grounds for him not wanting to say why we're having it, at least not yet, but I'm thinking it must involve yourselves?"

"That's true enough, but there are others involved as well. It wouldn't be right for me to break a confidence, and young Sean O'Halloran would never forgive me if he isn't allowed to make the special announcement after Mass next Sunday. He's been trying to worm information out of me all week! In fact," he added with an embarrassed grin, "Sean's persistent questioning is one of the reasons we fled the village for a few days, so we don't have to keep avoiding him."

Tommy roared with laughter at this. "Fair enough, Mr. McDermott! If you've arranged with Hugh O'Gara to keep certain things under wraps for a few days, I'm sure I can curb my curiosity until the weekend! If it's at all possible, I'll try to get over to Kilronan and Drumlion to wish yourselves, and the others involved, all the very best, whichever evening it turns out to be held."

Leaving the serving area, Tommy came out into the saloon area and walked with them to the door. Patting Gerald's neck, he produced an apple from somewhere or other and led the horse by the bridle strap to a spacious, well equipped stable behind the pub and helped Phil to unhitch the caravan.

He remained, nodding tacit approval of the way Phil took immediately to grooming the horse before seeing to his own comforts. A small boy—younger, Phil thought, than Jim or Sean —suddenly materialized with a bag of feed, and silently offered to take over the currying and grooming.

"Peter will never forgive you if you don't let him do the job," observed Tommy. Phil stood back and joined their host at the door, watching the youngster as he worked swiftly and confidently until Gerald's coat positively gleamed. "If you'd care to join us for general chat in the bar this evening, I'll do what I can to steer the conversation in a light and easy direction," offered Tommy as they crossed the yard back to the pub itself.

"We wouldn't want to impose," began Phil, but Tommy tutted impatiently.

"Sure, and we welcome visitors. If you knew how much we depend on the tourist trade, you'd understand that it's no imposition at all! And anyone who doesn't know your name already will know by this evening that there's a McDermott visiting Clogher, and they'll expect to see you and your good lady in the one place everyone visits most evenings!"

"Well, if you put it like that, I'd—or, rather, we'd be happy to oblige," replied Phil, with a swift glance in Kate's direction for confirmation.

"If nobody's mentioned it already, this is the nearest point for visiting the McDermott family vaults at Templeronan. Gerry, one of my regulars, can offer the use of his boat, and he tells a good tale of the known history, too!"

Phil blinked. "I'm sorry, the name—Templeronan?—hasn't been mentioned, so far. I didn't know there was a family vault. But I'd have thought the chapel on McDermott's Isle would have been the logical place for burials?"

"Gerry can tell you more about the reasons behind that. But I can say that, considering the number of clan chiefs, close family, and retainers who have needed burying in the family's long history, the vaults would have outgrown the chapel, and more than likely the Rock itself, long ago. The vaults are at Templeronan because it's not an island, with limited space available. It's on the banks of the river Shannon that runs down through Carrick, and it's easiest to get there by boat as the roads wander every which way. But as I said, old Gerry can tell a far better tale than myself, and he'll certainly be in tonight."

Gerry Hanrahan didn't appear to be as old as Hugh O'Gara, but they were certainly of the same generation and cut from the same cloth. Not "weathered," thought Phil, nor even that old clichéd term "weatherbeaten." Touched certainly by the years, but untouched by, even indifferent to, whatever weather he encountered seemed more accurate.

"*Sióchain teach*, Peace to the House," was his greeting as he entered, and it was evidently his custom. Those present nodded their thanks or raised a glass in his direction.

Easing himself onto a stool left vacant at the bar, he took a sip from the glass that Tommy had pulled as he entered, and nodded his approval. His gaze sought Phil's. "A warm welcome to our visitors. Not just everyday tourists passing through, or so I'm told!"

Phil offered his hand, which was accepted with vigor and enthusiasm. "The manager told me that you'd be the right person to speak to about some family research I'm working on."

"Did he now? And what makes Tommy McCardle so knowledgeable all of a sudden, I wonder?" The gentle dig was spoken in a manner which robbed it of all possible offense; the good-humoured twinkle in Gerry's eyes confirmed that this was simply normal village banter.

"I'd be obliged if I could arrange a boat trip for myself and Kate to a family vault at Templeronan. Mr. McCardle tells me that you may also be able to give me an outline of family history."

"So it's right then. You are of the McDermotts."

It could have been a question, but somehow, Phil didn't think of it as such. He nodded.

"I've already spoken to Hugh O'Gara about this. He seems to think the family line is straightforward, and what I can understand from Internet records seems to bear this out."

"So I've the honor of addressing *an MacDairmada*, I see! And after so long!"

Phil flushed. "I'm not trying to claim something that may not be mine!" he protested "But Hugh O'Gara and...and some other people..." He'd almost blurted out Paddy Ratner's name, but managed to stop himself. "And certain others," he continued after the briefest of pauses, "seem to think I'm at least close enough to claim the title, if I wish, though I understand it's purely an honorary title nowadays."

"Honor and tradition can be two sides of the same coin," observed Gerry, to nobody in particular. There was a general sigh of agreement, as if he had said something that struck the assembled afternoon drinkers as both deeply philosophical and unarguably true. "Still, I've nothing planned for the next several days. When would you like to go?"

Phil hadn't expected it to be so easy, but rallied his thoughts and they quickly agreed to make the journey the following morning. Further handshakes and a round of drinks sealed the bargain just as Tommy McCardle called over to Phil and Kate that their evening meal was ready, as soon as they cared to eat.

Chapter Twelve

Phil had brewed coffee and set out an extra cup to offer Gerry a wake-up call when he arrived.

Summer was drawing toward a leisurely close. A faint mist lay close to the riverbanks, and the warm glow resulting from the coffee was just what they all needed. Kate gave Gerald an extra large portion of the special malted grain Patsy Slattery had provided, and they strolled across to the footpath, which led down to the riverbank where Gerry had moored his rowboat.

Gerry eased the boat away from the bank, turning and using the oars to cross the current, allowing the river to carry them downstream.

"Is it far to Templeronan?"

"You'll be seeing it over my right shoulder as we come around the next bend. It's close enough, but on our way back, I'll likely thank you for some help on the oars pulling upstream."

With the ease that can only come from practice, Gerry sculled into a patch of dead water on the apex of the next bend in the river, and backed his oars to bring them to a temporary standstill mid-stream. On the opposite bank stood a low, rectangular, whitewashed building at the base of a gentle slope peppered with a fairly regular pattern of small, dark dots. As they drew nearer, these resolved themselves into a variety of grave markers, both in metal and in stone.

They hung for a few moments in mid-stream. Suddenly, Phil shivered violently and blinked, confused, looking around as if disoriented.

"What's the matter?" asked Kate, concerned.

Phil shook his head, as if trying to rid himself of the remnants of a dream, or even something more tangible such as the threads of a spider's web clinging to his hair. "Did you not hear the music? Or was it just my imagination?" he asked. Two pair of eyes stared back at him. Kate with evident anxiety, Gerry with a glance that more nearly resembled caution or reserve.

"'Did the bugles play the Last Post and Chorus?'" chanted Phil softly, and completed the couplet, "'Did the pipes play 'The Flowers of the Forest?'"

Kate recognized the lyrics of a folk song on a collection Phil had bought at a folk festival the previous year, a song about the futility and horror of war. She turned and explained this to Gerry. "I didn't hear anything, Phil, and as far as I can tell, Gerry heard nothing either!"

Gerry nodded his confirmation of this. Without comment, he laid into the oars again and began heading for the opposite bank, close to the building that Phil assumed had to be a chapel of sorts.

"It seemed so real," muttered Phil. "Just like being at the concert again."

This time it was Kate's turn to shiver. She turned and explained to Gerry. "It was only about a week or two after we saw the singer/songwriter who performed this song when we heard he'd been killed in a plane crash."

Gerry nodded. "Isn't it curious the number of musical giants who've been taken from us far too soon by accidents in recent years?" he said. It was almost as if he were thinking out loud rather than making conversation. "It all started with Buddy Holly, I suppose, or even Glenn Miller, though they never found a body, and some people still don't believe he died."

"Jim Croce."

"The Big Bopper."

"Jim Reeves."

"John Lennon."

Phil flushed. It had been completely accidental; his reference to Lennon's assassination alongside the documented accidental deaths of other musical legends was definitely out of place, but it was too late now to recall his words.

"'Tis indeed curious that we should come to talk of the deaths of musicians just now," commented Gerry as he plied the final few strokes needed to edge alongside a small jetty. "For it happens there's a tale to be told of a musician buried right here, who was famous the length and breadth of Ireland, though he never traveled very far from here during his lifetime."

"We'd love to hear it, Gerry!" said Kate, glancing briefly at Phil to enlist his agreement.

Gerry secured the painter to a convenient ring before replying. "If we take a short walk from here, I will show you his resting place. The tale of Mary McDermott, and her patronage of the blind Harper, Turlough O'Carolan, is one that would stir the most callous of hearts."

"Mary McDermott was the wife of Owen O'Rourke McDermott. He died when she was still quite young. She decided that she would continue to administer Moylurg in his name, as they had no children.

"At that time, almost three hundred years ago, there was a severe outbreak of plague throughout the land. The Kingdom of Tara, of which Moylurg was but a part, was severely affected. Of those who were infected, four out of every five died. Many of those who survived were left permanently disfigured or lame, to such an extent that they wished themselves dead. Some even took their own lives, unable to live with their handicaps.

"When Turlough was taken ill, he was a young man working on the estate, but at that time, he had not shown any aptitude for or interest in the study of music. He fainted and collapsed one day while at the main house. Mary McDermott, showing her true Christian compassion, showed no hesitation in having him carried to her private rooms, where she immediately had her own physician attend and examine him.

"When the plague was diagnosed, she ordered everyone except the physician and the servant who had carried Turlough to the room to leave at once, so that infection would not be spread. For the same reason, she also remained in the cottage. For three weeks they lived thus. Meals were brought by staff and left them outside the door to be collected.

"When the fever broke and Turlough no longer burned all over his blistered body, the physician removed the dressings and bandages from the worst wounds on his face and his upper arms. The wounds on his arms had healed over perfectly, but it was immediately evident when the dressings were removed from his face that the disease had left him blind.

"Turlough was a young man, accustomed to using his hands to earn his living. What was there left for him to do now he had lost his sight? For a full turn of the moon he was cast into a mood of the blackest despair, raging against his fate and the fickleness of fortune, which had robbed him of the means to make a living. He was also terrified of the thought that his mistress might turn him out of the house to beg or starve. But this was not in Mary McDermott's nature, and she resolved to bring him out of his dark misery. She began to read for him daily, or played on the lute and the recorder as the mood took her.

"Turlough responded immediately to her attempts to cheer him, and particularly enjoyed the music she played. Soon, he was humming along to the melodies, even extemporizing harmonies.

"One day, he asked her to allow him to hold the instrument she was playing, and show him where he should place his hands if he were to try to play on it. That day, she had been playing on a small lap harp. She stood behind him, placing his hands on the sound post and the strings, and Turlough immediately felt an affinity for the instrument. Without further prompting or instruction, he plucked several perfect chords on its strings. Mary sensed that he had a true talent that should be nurtured and developed.

"To his amazement and delight, Turlough discovered that his blindness was no hindrance in studying the harp. His senses of touch and hearing became far more finely tuned than those of a sighted person, until he became so much at one with his chosen instrument that he was scarcely aware of the loss of his eyes. Mary McDermott lost no time in commissioning Turlough a fine instrument of his own. Soon, he was composing original melodies on it, and writing pæans of lyrical praise commemorating the deeds of Tara's heroes, both living and dead.

"Turlough's reputation spread rapidly and soon reached the ears of Conor, who was King of Connaught at that time. He had heard tales of Mary McDermott's patronage of a blind harper and decided to see for himself. He arrived unannounced late one evening, asking for a night's sanctuary as if he were a common pilgrim heading for the shrine at Knock.

"He was greeted courteously and offered a simple meal in the kitchen, as the hour of the main evening meal was past. A servant escorted him to the dormitory reserved for travelers and they passed a door that was slightly ajar. Beautiful music and a powerful, emotional singing voice welled out of it, and Conor had to stop and listen.

"His guide paused and nodded, indicating that they might linger and listen for a while. Slipping through the door without needing to open it further, Conor stood, silent and amazed, in shadow at the back of the concert room. Turlough was engrossed in his music, as usual, and appeared unaware of the newcomers in the audience.

"As the ballad he was singing came to a final cadence, Turlough segued a short series of chords until he found a different key, and launched into one of his latest compositions. It was a ballad commemorating the prowess, skill, and bravery of Conor scoring the winning goal in a challenge hurling match against a team of fairy folk. It was a humorous song, full of laughing rills of melody and swift repartee. Long before the end, most of the audience were clapping rhythmically and joining in the refrain every time it returned. With a final flourish, Turlough rose and bowed to his audience, but appeared to stare with his sightless eyes exactly at Conor at the back of the hall and gave an extra deep bow in his direction before allowing his guide to lead him from the room.

"The following morning, Conor made his identity known to Mary McDermott, and thanked her for her hospitality. He took the opportunity to compliment her on her astute decision to support and protect Turlough O'Carolan. Without placing what might have been considered undue pressure on her, he made it clear that if she should ever feel herself in need of the protection of a strong arm, even consider marrying once more, he would be honored to be considered.

"Though flattered by the unexpected attention of her sovereign lord, Mary McDermott was more than capable of continuing to rule Moylurg unassisted. She had, after all, assisted her husband Owen with his duties for many years. She never re-married, however. She chose to devote her time and skills to caring for her protégé, Turlough O'Carolan.

"Neither of them could have known it, but when blind Master Harper Turlough O'Carolan died at almost seventy years of age—quite a creditable achievement, at that time!—he was also to be remembered as the last of Ireland's bards to be employed by a royal patron, or in this case, patroness!" They had strolled along the base of the hillock as Gerry told the tale, and begun to climb the gentle gradient. As he concluded the story, Gerry pointed with a gnarled walking stick. "We'll be heading off that way now, and I can show you Turlough O'Carolan's final resting place."

"After three hundred years, is it still possible to identify a headstone or memorial?"

"You'd be surprised, Kate. If you use quality stone and hire a master stonemason, the inscription will remain legible. And you can be certain that the grave of a heroic figure such as Turlough O'Carolan would be well-tended and kept over the years!"

Gerry paused at the top of the hill, next to a stone that was considerably bigger than those close by. It was also marked by a discreet row of ornamental metal railings no more than six inches in height. This was clearly a much later addition, probably no more than fifty years old. It had the effect of adding an extra dimension of honor and respect to the physical remains long turned to dust of the heroic personage buried there.

Crouching to scrutinize the lettering chiseled on the headstone, Phil could make out the name Turlough O'Carolan without difficulty. The lettering was larger and more deeply cut and was at the top of the stone. The rest of the text, however, was in an unfamiliar language, which he assumed had to be Gaelic. Gerry was right, though. Despite three centuries passage of time, it was still clear and legible.

"I can give you the nub o' what's written on the headstone," offered Gerry, "as I've taken my turn at tending the grave, same as most people in the village. But if you need an exact translation..." Phil was quick to assure him that this would not be necessary. Gerry nodded, and obliged with an approximation of the eulogy carved on the headstone.

"Turlough O'Carolan: blinded, you saw more clearly than most
God speed you, Harp Master
May you ever play your airs for the Heavenly Host"

Phil suddenly felt Kate lean against him, as if she were in danger of losing her balance.

He was just in time to support her with one hand under each elbow as she sank to her knees on the grass. He followed automatically, ending on his knees facing her. "Kate! What's the matter?"

"I just...felt a bit faint. The heat, perhaps. I don't know."

Phil placed his hand on the ground to support himself as he prepared to help Kate back to her feet. He looked at her curiously. "Did *you* hear the music this time?"

Kate was about to shake her head, but automatically grasped his elbow more securely. She frowned. "Just for a moment, I thought I heard something..."

"Describe what you thought you heard," suggested Gerry.

"It sounded like someone playing a guitar," Phil began.

"No! It was more like a piano, honky-tonk style, I think it's called!" Kate countered.

Gerry looked from one to the other. "Have either of you ever heard anyone play a harp?" he asked "Because if you haven't, I can understand why you can't agree whether it was a guitar or a piano."

Chapter Thirteen

"But why would either of us hear a harp? Or any sort of music, for that matter?"

They were back in Gerry's boat. Phil, as promised, was adding willing but inexpert assistance to Gerry with the oars as they pulled upstream, back to Kilronan.

Gerry gave a non-committal shrug of the shoulder. "Some things just are…the way they are," he grunted. "But nothing concerning one of the oldest septs of the Seven Ancient Kingdoms can surprise me anymore."

"How is it that you, and Hugh O'Gara, it seems, know so much about the history of my family? Is there a…connection? A blood relationship? Are we related somehow?"

Gerry took both oars once more, guiding the boat alongside the jetty. With a nod, he indicated that Phil should tie the painter to a convenient mooring ring. "If that were the case, Hugh would certainly be as honored as myself! But no, I'm afraid neither of us can claim family connections, other than our families have always been there for *an MacDairmada* and the Clan. Retainers, followers, supporters, call it what you will, from one generation to the next, we've been there whenever we were needed."

"You used a phrase I haven't heard before," said Kate as Gerry handed her out of the passenger seat. "You mentioned the 'oldest septs of the Seven Ancient Kingdoms,' and I'm afraid it threw me a bit! I can work out that a 'sept' is something like a family; 'kith and kin' might be closer, but I've never heard of the Seven Ancient Kingdoms before."

They strolled unhurriedly, three abreast with Gerry in the middle. There was no definite path or track from the riverbank back to the village, but the half-timbered frame of the pub was highly visible. Aiming for it, they ascended the gentle slope.

"The Seven Ancient Kingdoms of Ireland were already well established when the Book of Kells was begun, early in the ninth century. A king at the time was sovereign lord over as wide a realm as he could confidently say he had the military might to control.

"Moylurg was a part of the larger Kingdom of Tara, the largest and most powerful of the Seven Kingdoms. The area today is most of Roscommon, parts of Meath and almost the whole of Connaght, which, as I'm sure you can work out, takes its name from its most famous king, Conor.

"Conor had great confidence in his cousin Cormac MacDermot, whom he asked to rule in his name across Moylurg. Cormac performed the task gladly and with wisdom, and Conor rewarded this by making the sovereignty of Moylurg a gift *in perpetuum* to his cousin's family, a tradition that has continued unbroken ever since.

"The families Hanrahan and O'Gara have always been recorded as retainers or supporters of the Clan McDermott. Ask Hugh to show you his family crest. You'll see that it's a simplified version of the McDermott Coat of Arms!"

"Retainers?" Phil interrupted with a frown. "Isn't that a bit like...servants, serfs, or something of that nature?"

"Not really" Gerry assured him. "Though it sounds a bit old-fashioned, almost medieval, I suppose! But it's not a question of class difference, or master and servant. It's just the way it's always been, I suppose. Life moves at a different pace out here, as I'm sure you've noticed, even in the short time you've been amongst us!"

"That's true enough." Kate nodded. "And quite honestly, I much prefer the slower pace of life here."

Phil had to agree with her, and nodded to Gerry that he should continue.

"While there will always be people who move into and out of a community, certain families have always remained closely attached to this area. Now, it's barely within living memory that the last McDermott was obliged to move away from here, so you can appreciate that it caused not a little interest when we heard another of the name was coming to visit. Then, when you let it be known that you were researching family history, there was even more interest, and a lot of people have actually started speculating about whether you might be thinking seriously about staying."

His words seemed to float across the soft evening air as if they had been imbued with a life of their own, verbal butterflies of impeccable purity. The glade in which they stood was suddenly silent, as if it stood for a moment totally outside the flow of time, awaiting some signal before taking up the natural rhythm of existence once more. As he became aware of the temporal hiccup, Phil clearly heard a snatch of sweet music played by an unseen harpist. He shook himself from head to toe, resembling an overgrown pup who'd run indoors from a sudden shower of rain. Gerry didn't seem to be paying much attention, but he caught Kate giving him a curious look. He sent her a guarded stare, cautioning her to save her questions until they were alone. An almost imperceptible nod indicated that she understood.

Gerry was concentrating on rolling a cigarette and missed this glance between the co-conspirators.

"Now, there's more than a few amongst the village wondering...if it's not disrespectful to bring it to y'r attention..." He seemed reluctant to broach the subject he wished to discuss. To cover the gap, he pulled out a box of matches and lit his cigarette. "To be straight wit' yiz, there's many of us hoping that you'll decide to stay longer than the fortnight's holiday, and carry out, shall we call it, a more detailed research?"

He puffed strongly on his roll-up to cover his personal embarrassment. The glow seemed unnaturally bright in the rapidly fading daylight.

"Gerry, I can tell you straight away that Kate and I have already discussed this...in a roundabout, sort of fashion," Phil said reassuringly, and with a private grin that only Kate saw. Gerry's whole stance changed abruptly to that of a much more optimistic, confident man.

"Really? D'you know, Mr McD..."

"Phil, please! No formality while I'm on holiday!" Phil protested with a self-conscious laugh, which almost succeeded in covering his own embarrassment.

"Thank you! Phil, you probably don't realize just how important that news will be to everyone in the village. You've made a big impression on us all in a few days, so you have, and you'll be made very welcome by everyone!"

Gerry's relief was so patently genuine, Phil wouldn't have been surprised to see a troupe of cartoon leprechauns in green bowler hats dancing around the glade in celebration. A smile crossed his lips as this scene played itself across his imagination for a few seconds before he turned to more practical matters.

"Gerry, since Tommy's pub seems to be the center of everything of any importance that happens in Clogher, perhaps you'd be so good as to send out a message for anyone who isn't already there before us to...drop in for a few minutes, if they can spare the time?"

They had resumed their leisurely stroll from the quiet grove at the edge of the woods along the path that led to the village, and were now close to the pub entrance. The door stood open, beckoning, promising a warm welcome. Gerry looked around, but had no need to call for a messenger; young Sean appeared from nowhere. Gerry rippled a few words at him—Phil assumed it was in Gaelic, as he didn't understand any of it—and cuffed him gently on his way.

"There'll be people enough to listen to whatever you've a mind to say to them this evening, but I expect they'll wait until later on, and give you a chance to eat an evening meal before they drift along." His eyes twinkled as he said this. At the pub door, he bade them a courteous *au revoir* until later in the evening.

Chapter Fourteen

"I think that must be the first evening meal we've actually cooked all week," Kate said as she dried off the last of the cutlery and put everything in place.

"Yes, I noticed that too. I just hope we're not assuming too much, or... taking advantage of the generosity of people we meet."

Phil sat on a folding canvas stool next to the caravan with an opened bottle of white wine cooling in a pail of water as he waited for Kate to join him. He filled two glasses as she came down the steps, and they toasted each other in silence. The evening shadows were lengthening rapidly, and the only sound was the rhythmic *crunch-crunch* as an unseen Gerald made short work of the long, sweet grass somewhere on the far side of the caravan.

"I think the people we've met so far have been open and honest with us. I can't imagine them being, you know, two-faced, or insincere."

"Not really what I meant, Kate, but I'd hate to think we're being made into some sort of superhero figures, and sooner or later we'll be expected to...defend the honor of the Clan or some such impossible feat." Kate's carefree laughter was enough to dispel Phil's brooding thoughts, and he emptied his glass with a smile. "You're right, as usual. Sometimes I take myself too seriously. That's why I need you there, to laugh *at* me when I need it, as well as with me."

As Kate finished her wine, he leaned across to set aside her empty glass. Inevitably, the close contact became an embrace, and several blissful minutes passed before they rose, hand in hand, and headed for the lights of Tommy McCardle's pub and the reception they knew awaited them with the residents of Clogher.

As they entered the pub, Tommy McCardle nodded a greeting, then turned to one side and spoke a few words to someone behind him. Phil heard a door slam as Tommy gave them his full attention once more.

"I get no peace from young Peter if I don't allow him to brush and groom Ma Slattery's horses whenever someone rides past. He's been dancin' on his toes for the last hour or so! What's your pleasure, now?"

Phil was about to ask for two Guinness when he caught a tiny, discreet signal from Kate and amended the order to a pint and a half. Kate's arrived in a tall, elegant flute glass, complete with shamrock symbol drawn in the creamy head.

Phil looked around the décor of the room and was impressed. Where Michael Ashe's pub in Kilronan was festooned with musical instruments, which bore evidence of frequent use, this pub had seemingly been singled out as the local art gallery. Without overcrowding each other, scenes of country life intermingled with "head-and-shoulder" portraits—which he assumed were local dignitaries—on every wall except where glasses and bottles were kept on shelves behind the bar itself. Some of them he recognized as places they had already visited. This led him to guess that they were all local scenes, most likely the work of local artists. He turned to voice his thoughts to Kate, but she had already wandered off to inspect some of those closest at hand.

"Kate's a fine artist herself; she knows quality when she sees it," he said as he paid for the drinks. He tried desperately for a moment to remember what weekday it was. He was reasonably certain of his guess. "Is this typical for a Tuesday evening? Or are we early arrivals?"

They appeared to be the only patrons for the moment, but Tommy had already started a dozen or more pint glasses, each part-filled with Guinness.

"The time's not so important as the folk you're hoping to meet," said Tommy with just a hint of mirth in his voice. "What's most likely is, people wanted to be certain you'd grace us with your presence rather than just be passing through Clogher on y'r way somewhere grander. There, now!

What did I say? Peter will have been round the village before he even took a brush to your poor horse! You might find it a good idea to choose a table and sit yourselves before they all get taken. I believe you'll be making a lot of new friends and acquaintances before the night's over!"

Tommy's advice proved sound. Phil opted for a table with a clear view over the main room in front of an old-fashioned open fire, clearly the main form of heating for the pub during winter months. At this time of year, it was not in use, but had been scrupulously swept clean and was currently decorated with a mixture of dried flower arrangements and miniature portraits.

A continuous stream of people arrived alone and in small groups over the next hour. Some ordered their drinks at the bar first, others came to shake hands and introduce themselves, and Phil soon realized that it was going to be impossible to remember all the new names and faces.

"Yes, but it's more important that *we* know who *you* are!" was the comment of an older man who introduced himself as "of the O'Rourkes." This was at least a name Phil remembered having come across frequently in various books and writings, and was about to mention this snippet of information when the door opened once more. Automatically, every eye turned in that direction, and for a moment, all conversation faltered.

"*'Tis King Billy!*" murmured an elderly lady close to Phil's elbow. Was he mistaken, or had she made a furtive sign as she spoke the name, as if to avert an omen of some sort?

"A blessing on your beer, Tommy, if it's still as good as I remember it!" The newcomer hefted a small purse, which chimed with the heavy sound of coins. He was below average height, and probably past his half century, Phil guessed. Brown, knee-high boots suggested he rode rather than drove from place to place; grey-green jodhpurs tucked neatly into the boots reinforced this, and a black leather waistcoat with a thin layer of road dust completed the picture of a seasoned traveler. His jet black hair was carefully caught in a ponytail at the nape of his neck, topped off with a slightly crumpled felt hat, which reminded Phil of the chevron-shaped hats Hollywood generally reserved for films involving Robin of Lockwood and his arch-enemy the Sheriff of Nottingham.

"You're always welcome here, Billy; yourself and *all* your

family!"

Tommy continued topping up the next few glasses of porter as he spoke. Billy nodded politely, beat a few ounces of dust from his shoulders, and approached the bar. "If you'll do me the favor of telling me when we've drunk for what's in the purse, I've also some o' th' accursed folding paper folk use as means o' payment the day...you're busy tonight, I see?"

There was enough of a lift at the end of this sentence to make it unmistakeably a question, one which required a detailed answer. Tommy McCardle nodded sagely behind the bar as he flourished a trademark shamrock on the drink and placed it firmly in Billy's hand.

"As always, Billy, this first drink, for you and all your folk, is freely given, and on my personal slate! And while I'd never doubt but that you know the contents o' y'r purse to the nearest cent, I hope you'll allow one o' th' girls to tally it up in the back? My thanks indeed! And while I hope we'll have the pleasure of sharing some songs and music, as we always do on your all too seldom visits, you're right about being busy tonight, for it just so happens we've other visitors than your good selves, someone from far away and long ago, and someone I know you'll be glad to meet."

Phil sensed that Tommy, in his own unhurried manner, was setting out the chess pieces for a game of strategy that had to be played. Taking his cue from Tommy, he rose to his feet with glass in hand, and formally toasted the new arrival. Their eyes met and locked. Phil sensed curiosity tinged with surprise, but no animosity, not yet, anyway, and Phil felt the first hurdle, however small, had been negotiated.

"Phil, Kate, we are doubly honored this evening with the unexpected but most *welcome* presence of our traveling friend, Billy Lynch. How big's the family now, Billy?"

"Sure, and we manage to shake down each night in four vans, not that we couldn't make room for more, should it be needed."

He spoke slowly, and sincerely, but Phil sensed that the English he was using didn't come to him as naturally as the first language learned as a child should; it felt almost as if Billy was translating each phrase in his head before speaking the words aloud. Phil's gaze was still locked on Billy's across the intervening space of perhaps half a dozen strides. He made a decision, and took two steps forward with his free hand extended. Tommy McCardle, however, had not yet completed his introductions.

"Billy is what we in Clogher and other towns around Lough Cé are proud to call a genuine friend in need, a true King of the Traveling People. Billy, our guests this evening only arrived this morning, and I believe in some way you were destined to meet here tonight. This is Phil McDermott, and his lovely wife Katherine, visiting the area to research some family history, as I understand it?"

"That much is correct, Tommy." Phil nodded. "But we're also set on enjoying a holiday. We've owed it to ourselves for some time now!"

"So it's yourselves has hired one o' Patsy Slattery's fine, oiled and painted carts as is parked outside! No doubt you're drivin' around, thinkin' y'r livin' like *real* travelers? Am I right?"

For an instant, Phil faltered, uncertain how he ought to react. Was Billy's confident tone a gentle tease, or a direct challenge? And if it *was* a challenge, by what authority did "King" Billy feel he had the right to issue it?

Phil had a long, slow fuse and very rarely lost his temper. Between his second stride and the third, he made an instant decision to ignore the possibility that he was being tested, and continued to offer his hand in friendly greeting. "Mr. Lynch, I see you're both known and welcome here, and I'm the traveling stranger! Yes, we decided to hire the caravan from Mrs. Slattery because we thought it an ideal way to see something of Roscommon at a slow and easy pace. We wouldn't dream of comparing our holiday with the lifestyle of those who choose to travel the open road! Will you accept my hand on it?"

A gentle, almost inaudible sigh rippled around the room as Billy Lynch's face dissolved into a genuine smile and he pumped Phil's hand energetically. "Spoken soft, and like a true gentleman!" he declared, spinning round to address the room at large as he released Phil's hand. "Beware one and all! Here's a man whose tongue is a mighty weapon, one who can speak soft, yet drive a hard bargain when need be!"

When Billy turned to face Phil and Kate once more, he had, through some mysterious feat of *legerdemain,* acquired a full, foaming glass of Guinness. There were a few handclaps and subdued cheers from the room, followed by a slight shuffle as those on the closest tables tried valiantly to give Phil, Kate, and Billy the illusion of a degree of privacy at their table.

"Now, I have to wonder, is there maybe any one special reason you'd be researching into the history of such a well-known family name, and particularly in this part of Co. Roscommon?"

"I did a lot of research before we left Liverpool, Mr. Lynch."

"Billy."

"As long as you return the favour. Phil and Kate, agreed?" Phil continued in the same breath, rather than risk giving Billy the chance to protest. "What I read led me to this part of Roscommon, but what gave me the final pointer, believe it or not, was a certain estate agent's advertisement..."

By the time Phil and Kate had given King Billy a condensed version of the essential facts, three or four of Billy's entourage had arrived to join them. They sat cross-legged with their drinks on the floor at Billy's feet, speaking only when he spoke to them directly, and then only in short un-English phrases. Phil realized the language could just as easily be Romany as Gaelic, and he'd be none the wiser whichever he was told.

"So how are you going to make your dreams into reality?"

Phil's attention had wandered. He'd heard unmistakeable sounds of an *ad hoc* musical group tuning up. Any minute now...

The businesslike delivery of the question from King Billy left him in no doubt that it was posed as a serious question. Moreover, Billy evidently expected a serious and practical answer.

"As far as we've been able to trace the line, it appears that I was the first born male sibling in my generation of the family. I've one older cousin, Maureen, but..."

"Yes, the male side has precedence. That's the tradition, at least until or unless there isn't an obvious male link. So, I'll ask again, how are you planning to take your dreams—dreams you've *both* experienced, mark you—and turn them into reality? You *must* have been tempted to make plans, even if they only exist in your mind's eye."

The musicians at the far end of the room seemed to have

agreed on the tuning of their instruments and were seconds away from starting the evening's entertainment; further discussion would most likely not be possible.

"As I see it, Billy, the one thing stopping us is the asking price of the land. Three-quarter of a million Euros might be a very reasonable price for a whole island and everything that goes with it, but it's out of my price range, I'm afraid!" Phil laughed, but felt a definite twinge of sadness all the same. If only...

"*I heard that.*" Perfectly timed, Kate's distinct alto overlaying Billy gruff bass, the phrase echoed in stereo in Phil's ears. He shook his head in disbelief before looking left to Kate, then right to Billy for confirmation. Somehow, all three had somehow heard Phil's wistful plea fighting to survive.

"Somehow, Kate, we have to take this dream—"

"Hold it up against the wind, an' give it a slap on the rump!" suggested Billy

"*Then* decide what we want to do with it, and start to look around for where we'll find the cash to finance the project." Kate's practical *caveat* failed to take the gloss off the moment the decision had been made, a moment that they all recognized as soon as it had arrived.

Within minutes, without any formal announcement being made, everyone in the pub seemed to know what had been decided. Many toasts were drunk that night to mark the decision to buy and restore the castle, and Phil's word that he would present himself as candidate for the vacant title *an MacDairmada*.

Chapter Fifteen

Phil woke from a deep, natural sleep, knowing that the morning was not particularly advanced, and marveling at the fact that he really couldn't give a monkey's what time somebody in London had decided it should be. The world had not ceased to function since he had taken the decision to sideline his wristwatch.

Still, he had to concentrate before deciding that yes, this was Thursday. Turning on the radio for a time check, he became aware of soft voices and subdued sounds close by. The radio presenter announced the time to be just after eight-fifteen, and Phil realized that King Billy and his extended family were preparing to make an early start. He opened the door in time to see the last of the horses being backed up to the shafts of a caravan. Billy stood close by, and Phil realized that this was a semi-formal exchange of courtesies, as "between equals." It seemed that the self-styled King Billy had acknowledged his right to claim the vacant title of Clan Chief.

"I wasn't about to leave without giving the honor of an adieu, but when I heard you turn on the radio, I realized you'd be out afore long."

"Adieu, not goodbye, then? That pleases me too. I look forward to meeting again, and soon," Phil responded, moving forward to embrace Billy in an unashamed hug as used between close cousins, or those of unquestioned equal status.

"Our paths will cross several times, I'm thinking," Billy said, squeezing Phil's shoulders an extra time as they broke the embrace.

Phil frowned. "We've not that long left of our holiday."

"I think we both know this won't be the last time you grace these parts."

Billy's calm assurance as he spoke seemed to trigger something deep in Phil's thought processes. A subtle twist on the kaleidoscope of his mind's eye, and Phil saw the puzzle fall into place. The decision had been made

"I do believe you're right in that, though until now, I hadn't realized it myself." Phil grinned. "I'd be obliged if you'll carry a message from me—from us—for Hugh O'Gara when you reach Kilronan? I dare say he has a telephone, but I never thought to ask."

During general chat, it had emerged that Billy and his *caravanserai* were heading back along the same route Phil and Kate had decided to take, but in the opposite direction.

"My honor, and my pleasure to be of service."

"If you'd remind him of the worst-kept 'secret' of the week, and add that we hope you and your family will do us the honor of remaining a few days at Kilronan and attending the gathering planned for Sunday next?"

"Consider it done, and on behalf o' the family, I'll accept your kind invitation!"

With a whistle and a wave, four wagons were suddenly ready to roll. Billy bowed once more and hopped deftly aboard the lead caravan as it passed. A child jumped down from the last caravan to leave and secured the gate, leaving no visible sign there had ever been an overnight stop. The unmistakeable fragrance of fresh-brewed coffee intruded on Phil's deliberations, and he realized that Kate had risen and prepared breakfast while he was talking to Billy. The aroma set his digestive system on high alert, and he entered the caravan prepared to demolish several breakfasts, should they be available.

● ● ●

If Phil had hoped to be able to slide away from their first port of call without fuss or ceremony, he was disappointed. Even before they'd finished eating their breakfast, he'd noticed a few people making their way toward the pub, despite the early hour. Surely, now, Tommy McCardle wouldn't be serving alcohol at the back door at this time of day? He could only think of one other probable cause for such early traffic, and called to Kate.

"I'm going up to the pub to offer Tommy a night's rental, or camp fees, or whatever you want to call it. Care to come along? It looks as if there are a number of people wanting to press flesh before we get the chance to escape."

Once again, Phil had to deal with some stubborn resistance from Tommy McCardle before the landlord would accept any fee for their overnight stay, but he was prepared for this and had checked on his laptop for average rates at commercially run campsites. The exchange of bid and counter, offer and rebuttal, between Phil and Tommy quickly became a lively haggle witnessed by a jovial crowd, offering facetious and even semi-serious suggestions to the central debaters, supporting the one or the other as they danced like Olympic fencers, determined not to be outdone.

By the time he had beaten Tommy all the way up to what he considered the absolute minimum he could possibly pay for a night's stay, Phil was convinced that everyone who lived in Crogher had found an excuse to congregate at the village's nerve center in order to greet them and see them on their way.

"Well, I think they'll respect you the more for sticking to your guns." Kate joined Phil on the broad drive bench and handed him a mug of coffee.

"I still think Tommy should have let me give him a fair price," Phil grumbled, flicking the reins to remind Gerald that he was, at least theoretically, in charge. Other than the merest suggestion of a twitch in one ear, Gerald ignored the hint and continued to amble along at his own measured pace.

"Everyone enjoyed watching the pair of you squaring off, you know. I thought it was like seeing two politicians debating in the House."

"In some ways, it's a way of making your own entertainment when you live in an isolated village like Clogher."

They hadn't rushed to continue their journey, and Phil had made sure that everyone who wanted to speak to him had the opportunity to do so. The morning was well advanced before they eventually got under way, and it was close to midday. So far, they'd had the road entirely to themselves, with the sparkling waters of Lough Cé never more than a hundred meters distance on their right.

"Think we can make it as far as Knockvicar today?"

Kate picked up the map. "I'm no expert in reading maps, but there's only the one road that follows the curve of Lough Cé from Clogher, and we must be on it," she said. "It's pretty straight, just bearing slightly south—our right—close to Knockvicar."

"And that's the only bridge over the river Boyle, which we have to cross to get back to Kilronan," Phil added, dropping the reins in his lap and giving up all pretence of controlling Gerald's progress.

Reacting like a mischievous child who'd been waiting patiently for the most effective moment, Gerald threw back his head and half-reared between the shafts. Phil had to seize the reins as they started to slip off his knee.

Fortunately, they hadn't been in any hurry, so there was no damage to carriage or beast as the caravan shafts bumped gently against Gerald's rump and they came to a juddering but controlled halt. Despite Phil's best efforts, nothing would persuade their docile and amenable steed to take so much as one step further along the empty country lane.

"Something's spooked him, make no mistake, but what could it have been?"

Phil stood holding Gerald's bridle, which was soaking wet with spittle. He looked along the road in both directions, but saw nothing. At that moment, they could have been the only living souls in Co. Roscommon. The breeze had died to nothing; there wasn't so much as a chirrup from an unseen bird to disturb the silence of the land.

From her vantage point on the bench seat, Kate could see somewhat further and had an unobstructed view of the fields beyond the roadside hedges. "Those woods on our right, there's something running off in that direction. It's moving really fast, but it could have started from somewhere close to the road."

"Can't you make out what it is?"

"It's too far away to be certain, Phil, and it's moving very quickly too. It's also pure white, but not like any white I've ever seen in nature or in art! It's so bright it hurts to look at it!"

"Try to keep it in sight while I release Gerald and tether him in this field on the left. There's a stream close by, which will also be handy He's had a shock of some sort; there's no point in trying to force him take us any further today. This is as good a place as any to stop for the night anyway. We've plenty of supplies to make a scratch meal later on. Now, where's this weird whatsit you were telling me about?"

For answer, Kate pointed off to the right, more or less at a ninety degree angle to where they were parked in their now horseless carriage. "While it was still close enough for me to guess at what sort of animal it might be," Kate said with a slight frown on her face, "it seemed to be moving in a sort of a gallop, or canter, the sort of gait you associate with horses, I suppose."

"Big horse? Small horse? Pony? Even a deer, perhaps?"

"Not a big horse, not as huge as Gerald, for example. More like a pony in size, I suppose, though now you mention it, I suppose a deer would also be about the right size. Are there deer in Ireland? I know there are venison farms in England, but would they have them here, too, d'you suppose?"

"Let's go and see if we can get close enough to answer that. Of course, it *could* be a wild deer. I'm not convinced this is what I'd expect a farm field to look like. Oh, wait a moment!"

Phil had a sudden thought. "We won't be able to see the caravan behind this hedge. We need some sort of reference point so we can keep more or less on a straight path. Can you find a tea towel or something, and I'll see if we have something we can use for a flag staff."

Rummaging in the toolbox under the chassis produced a fishing rod, which was more than adequate for the purpose. On the field side of the hedge, just a few yards from the caravan, they soon came across fresh hoof prints heading toward the distant woods.

"From the space between them, it looks as if whatever it was took off at some speed. Look how far apart they are!"

"You didn't waste your time in the Boy Scouts either, did you?"

"*Touché.* I deserved that, but I wasn't making fun of you, Kate. Honest."

"Hmm. Come on then, O Mighty White Hunter, impress me by following the trail."

An occasional glance backwards at their makeshift flag kept them on course. The tracks seemed to continue more or less in a straight line, and at the top of a slight rise, just when they seemed to become more difficult to follow, Kate paused and held Phil back, plucking at his sleeve. Perhaps fifty feet ahead of them, a small shape lay, pulsating an incredible whiteness no artist's palette could match. It was so intense it seemed to glow in the bright afternoon sunlight, so pure it hurt the eye.

They stood a moment, transfixed, unsure what to do. The shape suddenly changed, and became a four-legged animal the size of a pony, or smaller. Perhaps it was a deer, thought Phil, but so impossibly white? The only tales he'd ever heard mentioning a white deer, or more precisely, a white hart, were legends and folk stories. It wasn't something one would expect to come across in real life. He realized that even the *shape* of the prints they'd followed had been too narrow and pointed to be made by any horse.

The albino deer/hart rose gracefully, presenting them with a view of its rump, complete with a short tail, which bristled with energy as it lashed from side to side. As if sensing their presence, the animal began to turn toward them.

The pulsing utter whiteness flowing from the animal took on a new aspect that could almost be felt, tasted. A vestige of professional raining caused Phil to slip his mobile phone out of his pocket and activate the video camera mode, but instinct screamed at him not to spook the animal with sudden noise or gesture. He waited, finger on button.

It turned unhurriedly, regally, to regard them with a pair of calm, violet-blue eyes, and Phil felt guilty, out of place, an unwelcome intruder, a poorly dressed peasant who dared to approach a regal presence.

Above the deep, wise, and unmistakeably ancient eyes hung a glorious coronet of fresh wild flowers; iris and buttercup, poppy and meadowsweet, lavender and clove, all surrounding a single large white rose. The coronet hung, incredibly, not from a set of antlers, but from a single spike the color and consistency of molten gold, which grew directly from the center of the beast's forehead.

The unicorn stared without fear at the couple, then glided on soundless hooves over the grass, directly toward Phil. It stopped perhaps three paces from him. He was vaguely aware of the fact that at some point, his thumb had activated the camera on his phone, though it must have been an automatic, unconscious decision motivated entirely by professional training and instinct. The camera was silent and unobtrusive, for which he was grateful. He hoped he would have a passable recording, as he dared not bring his left hand in front of his face to check the field of vision as he normally would have done. Nothing could be allowed to spoil this moment, this impossible meeting of man and myth in a very real, physical setting and in a country where legends were allowed to live on, untouched by modern life, society, or scientific proof of their non-existence.

The unicorn dropped its gaze in deference to Phil, as if it were acknowledging his superior rank and presence. It stretched forth its slender, graceful right leg, half-kneeling, and followed this by touching the ground before his feet with the tip of its horn, an unmistakeable gesture of salute.

Phil decided to risk raising the camera from waist level. As he did this, he felt emotions billowing from the unicorn, feelings so strong they were on the verge of taking on a definitive physical form. The strongest of them was...curiosity? Quite possibly. Mingled with pride, he decided, and including a healthy portion of hope. There was no question of the remotest trace of anything less positive. Somehow, he knew that the unicorn had no concept of any negative emotions, dark secrets, unworthy actions, or broken promises. It appeared as if this paragon of all things virtuous and undefiled was offering him its friendship and support, yet to what purpose Phil was unable to say or even to guess.

Holding his breath, Phil leaned fractionally forward without breaking eye contact. He had to force himself to believe that this was no dream as he slowly genuflected before the apparition, willing the beautiful creature to understand his wish to return the honor the unicorn had showed him by dipping its unique, golden horn to rest on the grass, almost touching his left boot. He continued to hold his mobile as steady as he could, and advanced his empty right hand toward the perfectly formed spiral before him. At the last possible second, he hesitated, gazing deeply into the unicorn's unfathomable gaze to beg for clear, unquestionable permission before daring to touch it. The unicorn gazed back at him, unblinking, inviting him.

He caressed the horn with the very tips of his fingers, feeling a thrill of energy surge up his arm and across his shoulders. The unicorn folded its forelegs to assume a kneeling position. Phil felt his hand, still in contact with the horn, being lifted as the creature lifted its head and touched the point of its horn first on his left shoulder, then his right in the manner of a king knighting a warrior.

Once the ceremony had ended, the unicorn rose to stand square on all fours once more, backing away slowly without turning or dropping eye contact After retreating half a dozen tiny, precise paces, it pirouetted gracefully to face the woods, perhaps thirty or forty yards away, and trotted without fuss or haste toward them without looking back. As it passed into the very edge of the first shadows of the forest, the incredible pulsating whiteness of its coat faded in an instant, as if a switch had been turned off, and there was no trace of the unicorn's further progress into the darker regions beyond the fringe.

"Should we even *try* to follow?" Kate had witnessed everything in silent disbelief. Her voice now sounded as if she was just beginning to learn a totally alien foreign language.

Phil thought about this for several moments before shaking his head. "I don't think so, Kate. Somehow, it'd be like...intruding, is that the word I want? On his—her?—privacy or personal space. We may get another chance, another opportunity, on another day, but for now...no, it just doesn't feel *right*."

"We'd better be pretty sure we can find this particular way into the woods if we're going to leave and come back another day."

"I guess there's nothing to stop us leaving a marker of some sort on the perimeter, something recognizable we can be sure will still be there tomorrow, or whenever we return."

"We'll have to be back soon, Phil. We've only three days left before we go home, and there's still the 'surprise' party we aren't supposed to know anything about."

"Point taken, it'll have to be tomorrow before we move on. That means we'll have to go into Knockvicar this evening and see if the local grapevine works as well here as it does in Clogher and Kilronan. We need any info we can get about local legends that might just happen to refer to...you *did* see everything I saw?"

"Check your mobile, Phil. You should have plenty of footage. But if you're referring to the unicorn, I saw it just as plain as you apparently did."

"We'd better leave a marker all the same. Think you can find the exact spot, Kate?"

"Still looking at it, Phil. I didn't want to lose track of where it just seemed to fade into the undergrowth."

"Brilliant! I've got a handkerchief I can tie on a bush; that should hold 'til tomorrow morning."

◉ ◉ ◉

It seemed cruel to put Gerald back between the shafts, and after checking on the map, they decided the walk into Knockvicar would do them no harm.

"It's less than a mile, I reckon," said Phil, "and we must have walked nearly that far to the woods and back."

Gerald's soft brown eyes were probably the deciding factor; he seemed almost to plead with Kate to allow him to stay in the field and recover.

"He's got you sussed," said Phil as they strolled off after giving Gerald a larger-than-usual helping of malted bran from the sack. "Those large, soulful eyes are a crafty con job if ever there was one!"

"Never mind, we've had very little exercise ourselves this holiday, and we're looking for some information as well as a drink, so don't forget your cassette recorder."

Following the road, which snaked along, shadowing the kinks and twists of the river, they caught their first glimpse of Knockvicar five minutes later as they topped a gentle incline.

"Looks like they've got a small harbor!"

"Yes, the tourist guidebook says lots of people come here for the boating on the Lough."

"Good chance of a bit of choice for somewhere cheap to eat then!"

"Bit late in the year for tourists, though, Phil."

"Maybe. We'll just have to take pot luck."

The first place they came to that offered both food and drink was faithfully set out in the style of a traditional Italian *trattoria*. The young waiter in the process of tidying a table as they approached was happy to serve them drinks *al fresco*, but with a glance at the evening sky, he suggested that they might want to consider moving indoors for their meal.

meal. The heat had already gone off the day, and Phil nodded his thanks for this practical suggestion.

"What does the guidebook say about this, Phil?"

They had been served their drinks, and a small selection of salted nuts, breadsticks, and olives had been brought with them. The waiter caught the startled expression on Phil's face, and hastened to assure them that this was perfectly normal in Italian restaurants, not an extra item on their bill.

Phil pulled the book out of his pocket. "It says that this is a genuine Italian restaurant with good quality food and excellent service, owned and run by a large Italian family. It says the service can sometimes be a bit slow, if it's busy, but well worth waiting for." He looked around. "At this time of the evening, unless there are already loads of people inside where we can't see them, I reckon we'll be okay for service—and anyway, we're in no hurry."

As they sipped their drinks, they studied the menus. Phil was relieved to see that they were printed in English underneath the Italian headlines, and there was also a third line of script, which by now he recognized as the flowing letters of Gaelic in a neat, green Italic font. He was pleasantly surprised when he realized that he had remembered enough of his schoolboy Latin lessons to work out what many of the Italian terms on the card meant.

When the waiter returned to take their orders, he nodded approvingly at their selections, and told them that the meal would be ready in about twenty minutes. With a swift look in Kate's direction for confirmation, Phil asked for two glasses of white wine while they waited and the rest of the bottle to follow with the meal. He declined the offer of a wine list.

"We're neither of us experts. If you choose something appropriate to the meal, I'm sure that will be fine."

The wine proved to be crisp, well chilled, and very dry, cleansing the Guinness from Phil's palate and leaving him ready to enjoy the meal as they were led inside and guided to a table where they could sit and examine the main restaurant for a few minutes. As expected, they were the first customers of the evening.

A set of hunting scenes were displayed on the walls of the alcove behind them, and the tags under each picture identified them as local scenes, not Italian: Boyle Abbey, Lough Key, Drumlion, and a number of other village names, places they hadn't yet had time to visit were amongst them. In each painting, the hunters were chasing deer.

"Oh, look!" said Kate, "In this one, they're after a white deer!"

"And that one, I can inform you, was painted not very far from Knockvicar, by a local artist, about a year ago...*prego, Signor, Signora*, enjoy your meal!"

The meal fully lived up to their expectations, and they luxuriated in being able to eat at a sedate pace and enjoy the ambience of the restaurant.

Phil made a note of the artist's name, and as he paid the bill, he asked the proprietor, who had come out to ask if they had enjoyed the meal, if there was any possibility of meeting the artist.

"Jack is well known in these parts, Signor, but he travels a lot of the time and I don't know if he's home at the moment. You might be best leaving a message for him at the Post Office. Most of the village trade is done there. It's also the local supermarket."

The last light faded from the sky as they arrived back at the wide bend in the road where they had parked the caravan.

"D'you know, all the time we've been here it's never even crossed my mind to worry about security, theft, or anything of that nature," Kate murmured.

Phil lifted her by the waist, kissed her tenderly, and placed her on the top step. "This isn't like watching your back every minute of the day, or wondering if your car will still be where you left it. I love my hometown, sweetheart, but there are things about it I definitely *won't* miss when..."

"When? Phil, do you mean that? You've decided to...?"

"Take up the challenge? Well, I suppose... Would it make you happy? Because that's what matters most for me, you know. As far as work's concerned, your art and my photography, it makes little difference where we're actually living, though it's a bit further to the nearest airport if I have to razz off on a job, but we can get around that."

"And look at the way that local artist, Jack..."

"Jack Bolam."

"Yes, well, he must have found some inspiration for his work from the fantastic scenery in this area."

"Maybe. Kate, you've just given me the germ of an idea!

We've made no plans for the future at all, yet. Nothing beyond somehow finding the funds to repair the chapel itself—"

"Which is going to be easier said than done," Kate interrupted, with a smile. "But go on, anyway. Suppose we get that far?"

"Humor me, suppose just that! Now, once that's been done, what do we actually *do* with the building? I mean, all that hard work, and then what? Okay, we've rescued what will no doubt prove to be a beautiful and historic building, but to what purpose? Somehow, we have to justify the money we put into restoring it. The building itself has to have some function, some purpose."

"Carry on. I can see you've got an idea, Phil."

"The chapel itself is the size of a couple of houses, and it's only a part of a much bigger building. We already know that."

"Yes, okay."

"So, we clear some ground around the chapel and add some basic housing. Kate, this is an opportunity to set up an artists' community with no outside distractions. It could be a place people can stay as long or as short a time as they feel the need, to concentrate on their chosen form of art—painting, sculpture, writing. We're close enough to Kilronan for supplies, and yet still isolated enough for people to experience the peace and solitude they might need to perfect their work."

"You're talking up a lot more funding than the original plan to restore the chapel, Phil, and you said it yourself, even *that* won't be cheap, or easy to finance!"

"One bridge at a time, sweetheart. Just tell me, would you go for the idea of establishing some sort of commune? Something like...oh, I don't know, Greenwich Village in New York or the *Rive Gauche* in Paris? A genuine artists' community?"

"It's got the advantage of bringing in some sort of income, I suppose. Even a token rent from the artists themselves would be more than just rebuilding the chapel and hoping enough tourists come by and pay for a guided tour."

"So do we go for it? I've already said I'm willing to the up the clan chief role everyone seems to expect of me. Now I need to know you're happy to accept that, and help build up a community. The island needs laughter, life, movement, bringing back to life!"

"I honestly think you've made the only possible choice, Phil, and I'm glad to follow your lead. Perhaps I'll see more of you between photo shoots than I have done the last year or so. At least we're away from the distractions of city life!"

A lingering, passionate kiss sealed the deal. Several minutes passed before Kate reluctantly had to surface for air. "I suggest you go and make sure Gerald's settled for the night while I brew us a last cuppa," she breathed. By now, it was almost full dark, and Phil had to stop and listen carefully to home in on the sound of running water before he stumbled across Gerald. A crescent moon hung over the treetops, giving him sufficient light to make out the silhouette of the caravan on his return journey, where coffee was ready to seal the end of an eventful day.

● ● ●

A return visit to the supermarket/Post Office was an unavoidable detour, of course. In such a small community, it was quite possible that someone had been in contact with Jack Bolam overnight, and there was even a chance that a reply of some sort might be waiting for them.

"We ought to support the local economy, and buy some snacks and drinks for the journey anyway," commented Phil as he parked the caravan.

"I vote crisps, and some *big* bottles of that gorgeous red lemonade," Kate replied.

"That's another good reason for coming back as soon as possible." Phil grinned as he looped Gerald's reins around a convenient lamp post. Hitching posts didn't seem to be a priority in the local town planning regulations.

The matriarch responsible for the smooth running of the emporium that seemed to be the village's sole supplier of everything and anything that could not be classified as alcoholic met them before they crossed the threshold, though they had hardly tried to disguise their arrival. Jack Bolam had indeed been contacted, and wasn't able to make it back to Knockvicar that day, but had promised to make a point of meeting up with them before they returned to Liverpool. Phil realized they'd have to be content with this, and turned his attention to more pressing matters. Fresh fruit, including apples as bribes for Gerald, were added to the shopping list, and after drinking the ubiquitous cup of strong, sweet tea, which had been poured as soon as they pulled up outside, Phil and Kate set out on the final leg of their trip around the Lough with the sun still respectably high, and the morning not too far advanced.

"If you want to spare y'r horse from hard trotting and the dangers o' main road traffic, you might cut through the Rockingham Demesne, just a mile or so down the road and on y'r right" had been their final piece of advice from an older man with a seasoned staff in his hand and a working dog circling his legs but never getting in the way. Crossbreed it undoubtedly was, but it was patently obvious that it understood every word spoken by the master.

"This must be it." Kate had the map, and pointed as she spoke. At the top of a slight rise was the unmistakeable silhouette of a fingerpost. One finger pointed directly ahead, naming a village that was large enough to be named on the map. The other read "Rockingham Demesne" and pointed off to the right along a well-maintained gravel path. There was a traditional five-bar gate to negotiate, but it was not padlocked. Kate jumped down to open it, and secured it again once Phil had passed.

"The sign didn't say how far either place is, but it looks as if we cut a mile or so by going through this...demesne? I ought to know that word, Phil. It sounds vaguely familiar?"

Phil thought a moment. "Demesne, domain. A matter of alternative spelling, perhaps? I think it's an old fashioned word for an estate, but *not* of the council type."

"Oh, more like 'Lord Derby's Estate,' you mean? Yes, that would make sense."

It was pleasantly cool under the canopy of leafy trees as they bowled along through the hottest part of the day. They passed slight widenings in the track every now and then, which would have been necessary if they had met another vehicle, but they seemed to have the road to themselves.

The woods, however, were full of life, bustle, and movement. Squirrels provided an impromptu gymnastic display over their heads. Kate saw one impudent grey deliberately drop a nut on Gerald's head. The familiar cooing of doves and pigeons contrasted sharply with the harsh croak of magpie and the faraway, sweet liquid voice of the skylark as he ascended once more to an impossible, dizzying height without becoming inaudible.

The undergrowth on each side of the track also teemed with wildlife, seemingly totally unafraid of the creaking, swaying wagon and its passengers. Rabbits sat and watched them thoughtfully, nibbling on the grass of the narrow verges. Just too far away to be identified, a large bird burst out of a bush and spread its wings in a running take off. A split second later, a fox followed at a dead run, jaws snapping uselessly on thin air as the bird—Kate thought it might have been a pheasant—achieved flight.

"We wouldn't have seen *any* of this if we'd stayed on the main road!" she said as she poured two large tumblers of red lemonade and passed one to Phil.

As he drew breath to reply, the whole forest became instantly and completely silent. The *clip-clop* of Gerald's hooves, an insignificant detail against the normal background hum from the forest, immediately became unbearably loud. With no conscious signal or effort from Phil, Gerald's steady pace faltered. After no more than half a dozen paces, he stood completely still.

The least of all possible stirrings in the very corner of Phil's field of vision resolved itself into the unicorn, standing four-square, unafraid, in the center of the track. Had it in some strange, magical fashion managed to appear there? Or had it stepped from behind a bush while they were looking in a slightly different direction? The next corner was too far away for it to have hidden *there*, waiting.

For two, perhaps three seconds there was neither sound nor movement, then the unicorn's nostrils flared slightly, and the vision slowly folded its forelegs in a formal bow of obeisance. As it rose again, an audible sigh rippled through the forest, as if the whole of nature had been holding its breath for the duration of this special moment. Kate noticed the top boughs of the trees whipping back and forth, though there was no breeze to speak of. Phil was also distracted enough to glance to one side at the unexpected return of the day's ordinary background noises, and when they looked at the road again a split second later, the unicorn was gone.

"It was kneeling to *you*, Phil!" Kate whispered, a mixture of wonder and perhaps just a little fear in her voice. "The unicorn knelt to *you*!"

Phil drove Gerald more firmly once they restarted, and the horse didn't complain at the sudden demand for extra speed. Soon the track joined a wider, tarmac road, which led them to the main entry and exit of the Lough Cé Country Park. A brief consultation of the map to orient himself, and Phil turned right onto the N4. Less than a kilometer away, the village of Kilronan was a welcome sight. Gerald evidently agreed, and needed no further encouragement from Phil to kick up his heels and head for the stables behind Michael Ashe's Pub.

Sean, pot-boy and general gofer, was the only resident to witness their arrival, or at least he was the only person Phil and Kate saw as they arrived, though they hadn't tried to sneak in. Gerald was by now blowing hard, and the wagon seemed to have acquired a whole vocabulary of extra loud groans, janglings, and clashes since their unscheduled halt in the depths of the forest and Gerald's subsequent efforts to get them back as quickly as possible.

A €10 note appeared for a nanosecond in Phil's hand before disappearing just as swiftly into Sean's pocket.

"I want you to give Gerald the *best* rubdown of his life. Can you do that?"

He nodded.

"He's had a bit of a strange day, and worked very hard. If I promise to tell you *everything* later on when we've a moment, will you promise not to say anything to anyone without my say-so? It's important, Sean. *Very* important!"

"Sure, an' you're the boss, Mr. M...*Uncle* Phil!" he corrected himself as he began to unbuckle the harness. "I'll look after this old rascal, so I will! And I'll not let anyone else *near* him, not even inside the stables until I'm done with the job!"

Gerald was led away. Phil heard a solid *thunk* as a heavy wooden bar was dropped in place to prevent the stable door being opened from the outside, and he grinned to himself. Sean was taking no chances of being caught unawares performing his grooming duties.

Chapter Sixteen

"So it's yourself, then. Did you have a pleasant trip?"

"Yes, thanks, Michael, and we managed to avoid a lot of awkward questions as well! Has young Sean been behaving himself?"

"He's done all his jobs well, and quicker than usual. He's also been all round the village asking questions, but as far as I know, your secret's still safe!"

"And the jeweler, Mr. Ratzner? Has he—"

"Brought the rings himself just this morning. Would you like to try them on?"

"They've always fit well, but I'd like to see them with the *claddagh* mounted."

Michael reached under the bar and brought out a small parcel, gift wrapped and ribboned. Inside it, two rings sat side by side on a velvet cushion, buffed and polished, a perfect color match to the added adornments.

"I'd never have known the *claddagh* were mounted at a later date. They're perfect!" exclaimed Kate.

"Worth every penny. The man's a master jeweler." Phil nodded.

There was just time to replace them in their box before the door swung open and the first evening regulars arrived to slake their thirsts. Michael topped off two glasses for Phil and Kate before leaving them to attend to the new customers.

Everyone who entered sooner or later came across to where Phil and Kate sat at a corner table to greet them and ask about the trip around the lough. The grapevine had evidently been at work, and the chance meeting with King Billy was common knowledge.

Most people seemed to agree that Billy Lynch was a wise one who knew a lot more than people generally gave him credit for, and had his own reliable sources of information, which at times were impossible to explain.

There was a brief stir behind the bar, and someone entered from the kitchen area carrying Kate's sketch, glazed and mounted in a neatly dovetailed frame of some pale wood. This was given pride of place—to a tumultuous, spontaneous and sincere round of applause—on the wall behind the serving area. Kate had almost forgotten about it, and was embarrassed to think that someone had gone to such lengths to mount her sketch in such a beautiful frame, but had to accept the gift in the spirit it was being offered. Several people tried to claim the honor of buying the next round of drinks, but Phil decided the time had come to be firm.

"We haven't had the chance to groom our horse yet today," he insisted, "and I promised Patsy Slattery we'd look after him."

⚙ ⚙ ⚙

"Well *I* think they'll respect you more for sticking to your guns!"

They were back in the caravan and Kate was preparing the percolator. Phil paused then shrugged before lighting the stove. "It's still the truth," he retorted. "We've been far too slipshod about grooming Gerald. Remember what Patsy said about keeping him working so he doesn't get fat and lazy?"

"It was just an excuse, and don't think you can fool me, Phil McDermott, not after all this time. Apart from anything else, I heard you bribing young Sean to give Gerald an extra-careful grooming when we arrived, and I'm certain money changed hands. You had a 'moment' back there in the bar, of that much I'm certain. Now, spill."

Phil placed the pan of water on the gas flame and sat back, conceding the fact that Kate had spotted his fey mood as accurately as ever. In fact, he didn't think she'd missed a single one—and there had been a number of them—all the time they'd been on holiday. When he thought about it, they were starting to happen more and more frequently. It could only be because he was so much more relaxed than usual, he told himself. It had never occurred to him, or Kate, for that matter, to question the ease with which they both accepted the fact that they had always shared such "moments." Throughout the years they'd known each other, there had been frequent occasions when one or other would feel or sense something with a certainty that defied explanation. When they started jotting down times and thoughts in separate notebooks, they discovered that they often had similar, powerful "moments' even when they were geographically far from each other. They quickly agreed not to mention this to any of their colleagues. Anyone who had not experienced it themselves would be likely to consider them self-deluding charlatans. It had the effect, however, of cementing their relationship, binding them even closer, if that were truly possible.

Kate set aside the percolator and sidled close, cupping the palms of her hands around Phil's elbows, drawing closer, relaxing into his arms.

"It never ceases to amaze me how well you know what makes me tick," he murmured, nuzzling her forehead, stroking her hair.

Kate nodded. "I can tell you exactly when it happened. It was while Gerry was rolling his cigarette, and then there was a 'replay' moment just after he lit it. Am I right?" She didn't even wait for confirmation, but carried on as if Phil had answered. "So, out with it. Tell me what you...I'm going to say *heard* rather than saw. I'm right again, aren't I? I just couldn't tune in properly this time."

Phil took a half stride back and raised both hands in mock-surrender. "Okay, I give in."

He thought about the best way to describe what he'd experienced in the space of a few fleeting seconds. "I gather neither you nor Gerry heard...what I heard again?"

He paused and looked intently at Kate.

She shook her head. "I certainly didn't, and I'm sure Gerry would have commented if he'd heard anything. Was it the same? Harp music?"

"Now I know what a harp's supposed to sound like, I can say yes to that. What I can't figure is why am I the only one who seems able to hear it?"

"You aren't completely on your own. Remember, I heard

something on at least the one occasion, and I think Gerry heard it, too."

Phil put his coffee down untasted. "Just pass me that guitar. I want to see if I can at least get the melody line off pat before I forget it. The chords can wait until I've more time."

After a few false starts, he managed to string together something that he thought was a fair approximation of the ethereal, haunting melody he'd heard.

"I never thought I'd be cussing myself for not bringing a supply of manuscript with me, but composing tunes, or even recreating them from memory, was probably the last thing I expected to find myself doing on this holiday," he said as he ran through the melody once more before attempting to make a recording on the cassette recorder they'd been using for interviews.

"You can't think of everything, Phil. I wish you weren't so hard on yourself sometimes," Kate replied. She frowned, concerned, as she saw the lines of concentration on his forehead. She added gently, "You shouldn't be working so hard. This was supposed to be a *holiday* as well as a research trip, remember?"

For answer, Phil's right hand moved away from the guitar and curled round the back of Kate's neck, drawing her face down gently into kissable range. Within seconds, she was on his knee. The guitar stood idle, precariously propped against a fortuitously placed stool, dumb witness to a "holiday moment."

When they eventually surfaced for air, Kate rose and straightened her clothing, touching Phil tenderly on top of his head as he remained seated. A tacit glance toward the cramped zone grandly described as the cooking area at the rear end of the caravan indicated her immediate intentions. Phil nodded, and turned his attention once more to capturing the remembered skeins of melody in a more permanent form.

Kate bustled backwards and forwards, juggling pots, pans, and plates while Phil hunched over his guitar and concentrated on his self-appointed task. Kate listened with more than half an ear as he played phrases over and over again until he was satisfied. She thought of his capacity to soak up melodies, spongelike, as a miracle, something she could never hope to emulate. It never occurred to her that, as far as Phil was concerned, her ability to create accurate, lifelike sketches at the drop of a hat was no less of an achievement, something he would never be able to master.

With a nod and a *sotto voce* "Yes!" which he was patently not aware of uttering, Phil hit the stop button on the cassette recorder, knowing even before he rewound it to listen to the result that it would be acceptable. As it came to an end, Kate slid two plates onto the table.

"Mmmm! Bangers and...mash?" queried Phil. The sausage was unmistakeable, but the mash looked a bit different somehow, flecked with something giving it a greenish tinge.

"Not quite, but close," laughed Kate. "Moira suggested I do something a bit different. This is an Irish recipe called Culcannon. There's shredded cabbage mixed in it, and a bit of onion. Plus, the gravy's special too!" She put two tumblers on the table and produced an open bottle of Guinness from the cooking area, splitting it equally between the glasses. "She told me to add a generous splash of this to the stock water and split the rest of the bottle between us," she said with a laugh as she sat down. "Come on, let's eat while it's hot!"

🌀 🌀 🌀

After they had eaten and tidied away, Kate wandered out to the stable, intending to give Gerald a thorough grooming and an apple. This gave Phil a bit of space and time to carry out some largely cosmetic polishing of the recorded melody, which he suspected would prove to be another of Turlough O'Carolan's works. The energy and effort she put into the exercise left her feeling good about herself, as well as salving her conscience about not grooming the horse as often as she'd intended during their holiday.

As she fed Gerald a second apple, Phil entered the stable with the cassette recorder slung over his shoulder.

"Ready?"

"Mmmmnn. Guess so! I think he's sussed out that's all he's getting, and Patsy Slattery *did*
   warn us against overdoing it."

Neither of them believed Patsy's dire warnings against spoiling Gerald, but they were anxious to move across the courtyard into the pub itself. They were both looking forward to spending the evening discussing matters with the local community, matters which they sensed could very easily become a major staging post in their lives.

Though it still wanted a few minutes before seven o'clock, they were far from being amongst the first arrivals in the bar, where Michael Ashe as usual held court. They were greeted on arrival as if they were long-term permanent residents of Kilronan and made to feel genuinely welcome. Kate took the cassette recorder from Phil and claimed a still-vacant table close to the central hearth in the center of the rear wall of the building, where she remembered seeing a power point she could commandeer.

At the bar, Phil accepted the glasses offered him and left a substantial tab to go behind the bar toward the general village thirst. By the time he joined Kate at the table, several more villagers had arrived and Moira was kept busy circulating the pub, replenishing glasses. Michael Ashe kept up a constant stream of fresh pints and ancient jokes for the entertainment of those who preferred to stand at the bar.

A ripple of anticipation soughed through the room as the door opened and closed once more, admitting the august presence of Father Tomàs Costello.

"*Síochán sa teach!* Peace to the house!" he intoned as he crossed the floor, acknowledging a sprinkling of replies. These lay just beyond Phil's intuition to guess at the meaning of them, but they were evidently along the lines of a "same to you" reply.

Michael Ashe pushed a glass in his direction. Father Tomàs nodded his thanks, but before taking it, he turned and glanced around the room, which instantly fell silent.

"*In ainm an Athar agus an Mhic agus an spioraid Naoimh.* In the Name of the Father..." he said, and with an easy gesture, gave a general blessing to all those present. In response, foreheads, hearts, and shoulders were automatically touched. He made his way to the table where Phil and Kate were sitting, one eyebrow lifted in silent inquiry before he sat on the last remaining free seat in the pub. By some miracle, three pints of Guinness and three shot glasses filled with clear, amber liquid had appeared on the table while everyone's attention had been elsewhere. Moira was conveniently a few tables further down the room with her back to Phil, impervious to the ferocity of his stare as she wiped tables and replaced empty glasses with full ones.

Father Tomàs waited until the room had settled and he had everyone's attention.

"First of all, in order to keep this meeting as relaxed and informal as possible, I'd like to address the pair o' you as Phil and Kate rather than Mr. and Mrs. McDermott. Everyone else in the room's on first name terms, and I hope you'll not take it amiss?"

With a swift glance, Phil answered for both. "Only too happy, Father. And can I save time by saying straight away that I'd like to record what's said this evening? I may have to follow up some of the points we touch upon tonight, and I've a memory like a sieve." He grinned at this exaggerated piece of self-criticism, and was pleased to see from the general reaction that people took it in the good-humoured spirit in which it had been intended.

A few seconds of muted neighbor-to-neighbor gossip followed, and when Michael Ashe called for a show of hands, there was as close to unanimous approval as made no difference.

Father Costello took the initiative. "Phil, Kate. We're close to the end of your fortnight's stay amongst us, and I sincerely hope you've enjoyed yourselves and taken some opportunity for a *proper* holiday, as well as all the hard work, traveling, and research I know you've been doing. I know I speak for us all when I say it's been a pleasure to meet the pair o'you!"

This pronouncement released an instant, spontaneous murmur of genuine approval from the room. Both Phil and Kate flushed with unwonted embarrassment at the unexpected compliment, and Father Tomàs continued.

"There are a number of things we all feel need to be mentioned before you leave us, even if it's true what I've heard, and you plan to be back with us on a permanent basis before too long?" He paused for a second and looked around the room before he added, "For example, there are things you have the right to know about if you're thinking of assuming the responsibilities of the title *an MacDairmada*."

A hush settled on the room. This was the first time the subject had been broached at an open, public gather of any sort, or at least it was the first occasion Phil was aware of. Acutely aware that he was the only person with any right to speak on the subject, he stood up. Placing his Guinness on the table and his hands on his hips, he addressed the question implicit in Fr. Costello's softly spoken words. Although he had made no notes or other preparations, he found that the words he needed came to him fluently and naturally.

"It's true that when Kate and I arrived, we were following a whim, chasing something that we'd stumbled across, which seemed at the time like pure coincidence." He warmed to his theme, speaking as fluently as a professional after-dinner speaker accustomed to spending hours before a mirror perfecting a speech. The sincerity behind every word carried conviction

"Some of you, most of you, probably, will know that one of the reasons we came here was because Kate had been troubled for months on end by a series of troubled dreams. Now, just for the record..." He paused for a moment to give his next words their full effect. "I know that there are probably some of you who'll doubt this, but Kate herself will tell you that she hasn't had a single night of broken sleep since we arrived."

All attention was immediately transferred to Kate, who stood and nodded her agreement.

Phil moved a half-step away from Kate and the tableau resolved itself. Everyone's attention was back upon him, and Kate was allowed to seat herself once more.

"There are still a lot of things neither of us can understand nor explain, but we feel we've learned enough to take certain things on trust and assume they'll eventually resolve themselves if it's really important that a logical explanation of some sort is required."

This statement sparked a brief, general debate, which to Phil sounded positive, even optimistic in tone, even though at least half the murmured conversations were carried out in Gaelic. An older man standing at the bar caught Phil's attention, and made his comment through the "Chair" in the form of Father Tomàs.

"Have you given our guests some idea of what goes with the title *an MacDairmada*?"

"Brendan, you raise a fair point," the priest conceded. "Phil, I leave it to you."

"Thank you, Father, and you too, Brendan..."

"O'Hanlon."

"Thank you for that, and for the question. It's only fair

that everyone should know exactly where we stand on this and several other important points. I have to admit, I knew very little before we arrived, and I'm sure I've only scratched the surface of what I need to learn if I'm to make a good job of what I intend because the short answer is, yes. I *do* intend to apply for the vacant title, and the responsibilities that follow hand-in-glove, if you're prepared to have me here. In fact," he added, suddenly certain that it was the right thing to do, "Brendan, I'd be very happy to have your assistance, if you're able to meet with myself, Father Costello and Hugh O'Gara to discuss such things tomorrow lunchtime?"

The gleam of unqualified respect and approval in Brendan's eyes confirmed the accuracy of Phil's assessment of the situation, even before he agreed to the suggestion.

Phil reached down to the table behind him and came up with the small shot glass, raising it so that its amber contents caught the reflections of the overhead lighting and seemed to sparkle with an inner life of its own. "*Sláinte!*" He had heard the word often enough, and was confident he could pronounce it correctly.

He needn't have worried. The assembly rose to their feet, each raising a glass in response. "*Sláinte!*" came from perhaps half a hundred sincere, thirsty throats, and spontaneous applause rippled around the room.

When everyone had settled in their places again, Phil sensed that it was most practical if he took a tour around the room to shake the hands of as many people as he could, rather than expect them to come to him. It took him the best part of half an hour to circulate and press the required amount of flesh. When he returned to his table, there were fresh supplies of an alcoholic nature waiting.

"You're somewhat behind, I'm thinking," teased Father Tomàs as he saw Phil's expression.

"Nothing I can't get to grips with!" retorted Phil. In truth, though he was generally no more than a moderate drinker, he'd noticed his ability to put Guinness away had improved considerably over the fortnight. He decided this was probably due to the drink being served with far less gas behind it than was generally the case in an English pub.

A thought came to him as he replaced his glass on the table. Reaching in his pocket, he took out a different cassette and popped the recorded cassette from the machine. With his gaze on Kate, he said, "Father, I'd like to play you something we...no, let's be honest about it. Something *I* heard while I was out with Kate and Gerry this afternoon, just before we got back here to Kilronan. While we were at Templeronan, the family crypt, I heard something else and both Kate and Gerry said they heard something, but this was, as far as I know, something only I heard."

By the time he'd finished this introduction, there was a growing crowd of interested parties gravitating toward their table as word rapidly spread that Phil had more entertainment to share.

As the first notes Phil had reproduced on his guitar made themselves heard, all conversation faltered and ceased for a second time that evening. As the music drew to a close, it seemed as if everyone held his or her breath, desperately hoping that the haunting music might continue just a little longer. A respectful silence lingered for several seconds until Phil ended the low hiss of blank tape with a preternaturally loud *click* on the stop button.

"Let us hear that again, if you will," breathed Father Tomàs, as if he scarcely dared disturb the silence that had become almost palpable it lay so heavy. Other voices concurred, encouraging Phil to follow the priest's suggestion.

This time, a tapping foot somewhere close to the bar laid down a steady, rhythmic beat, which was swiftly copied by a *bodhràn* drum. Before the ending of the first phrase, a flute or a penny whistle had joined in, and from the corner of his eye, Phil saw an arm raised to take down a fiddle from the wide range of instruments displayed around the pub. Hums, hand clappings, and even the slightly off-key notes of a perfectly in-tune banjo completed the range of instruments that supported or complemented the single melody line Phil had picked out on his guitar. The tape came to an end, but the musicians took little notice, extemporizing, decorating the basic melody with personal variations of their own invention. After a third and even more involved, contrapuntal verse had been added, the musicians came to a satisfying conclusion and all managed to finish within half a beat of each other's timing.

"That was...very impressive!" was Phil's first comment. Inwardly, he winced. His words, in his own ears, sounded somehow insincere at best, possibly even patronizing or sarcastic. He felt his whole body tense as he waited for a reaction from the room.

The reaction took him completely by surprise. A thunder of spontaneous applause and cheers splintered the brief silence, which ensued as the final notes died away. Father Tomàs' lips moved briefly, but Phil couldn't hear what was being said.

"Phil? Are you alright?"

"I'm sorry, Father, I was woolgathering. What was it you said?"

"That's alright, my son. Now, tell me, did you know that was more or less exactly and to the note a longer piece Turlough O'Carolan wrote toward the end of his life? In fact, it's one of the few pieces that holds up well when played as an orchestral piece rather than a harp solo, or with an orchestra behind a harp soloist."

Suddenly, it became crystal clear for Phil why it had sounded so right to have the others playing an accompaniment behind the soloist. O'Carolan had *intended* the harp to be accompanied by other instruments!

"Might I inquire if the piece has a name, Father?"

"Sure, and 'tis called *Carolan's Concerto*, one of his finest pieces and one of the most difficult to play."

Phil frowned then shook his head in disbelief. "Pardon me, Father, but if it's reckoned a difficult piece to play, why does it sound so..."

"Natural when it's played? Is that what you're asking?"

Phil nodded.

Father Tomàs leaned back in his chair and swept the room with a glance. "Now, I'm not musically inclined myself, you understand, but I'm thinking that those who joined in this evening have all played the piece before on one instrument or another, so I've no doubt they're used to improvising a backing to a strong lead solo such as they had from the tape you played."

Wordless mumblings of general agreement from the room confirmed the accuracy of the priest's assessment.

"You mean, that was more or less 'off the cuff'—unrehearsed?" Phil was even more impressed by this than he had been by the quality of the music itself. "Do you suppose it would be possible to..." He gestured mutely toward the recorder, and waved a spare cassette in the air. He needn't have worried, the musicians were well lubricated, and keen to experiment further with extemporizations

"But we'll thank you to join in yourself rather than play the tape!" came an unidentified voice from the rear. Phil was only too happy to oblige. Kate did what she did best, which was to run the recorder and coax the best possible sound quality out of very basic equipment.

She was suddenly aware of young Sean, silent at her elbow, with eyes on stalks as he observed the tiny, delicate adjustments she was making on the volume controls with her long, slim artist's fingers. She grinned self-consciously. "It's not that difficult, you know. It's not like a pro mixing desk where I could beef it up to sound like a studio recording."

Sean sighed and shook his head. "I'm sure you're right. It's just that, you know, in a small village like Kilronan..." He stopped, evidently embarrassed.

Kate took pity on him. "You mean you haven't the chance to mess about with things such as...let's see, would I be far wrong if I guessed cameras and recording systems are first on your personal list?"

Tongue-tied, Sean nodded silently.

"Well, listen, now. In a few years' time, when you're thinking about school exams and what you're going to do with yourself, if there's a way Phil and I can help you find a college, or a course, or something? Then all you have to do is ask! Deal?"

For a second, Kate wondered if she might have gone too far. Sean flushed beetroot red from his throat upwards, enhancing his densely-packed freckles until they resembled a terminal case of smallpox. At the same time, his eyes flooded with tears of gratitude, and with a nod and a mumble of thanks, he fled to the kitchen, or possibly the stable yard behind the pub, where he could give way to his emotions unobserved.

A majority decision amongst the musicians indicated that the recording session had reached a satisfactory conclusion. As the group rose from their seats and stretched, Phil moved across to sit next to Kate.

"Is Sean alright? What's upset him?"

Kate explained, and added, "I didn't think he'd take it like that, though, and I hope I haven't hurt his feelings."

"He looked more embarrassed that upset, to be honest,"

Phil replied thoughtfully. "I'll just stroll out there and make sure he's okay, shall I? Won't be long."

He found the lad in the stables, and quickly reassured him that what Kate had offered was, in *both* their opinions, neither more nor less than Sean had earned already. This man-to-man discussion was just what was needed to restore Sean's self-esteem. He went back to grooming Gerald in a much better frame of mind.

After the customary singing of the national anthem, Kate and Phil automatically started carrying empty and unfinished glasses to the bar for Michael Ashe to wash.

Michael caught Phil's eye. "That was well handled. What did you say to young Sean?"

Phil explained briefly.

Michael Ashe nodded his approval. "He's a bright one and no mistake. It won't surprise me if he takes an opportunity to better himself through higher education of one sort or another when the time comes," he said as he polished a final glass and set it in place. "Will you join us over a final glass afore ye leave?"

Glancing toward the snug, where Michael had indicated with a glance, Phil saw that Hugh O'Gara and Brendan O'Halloran were sitting with Kate, who had tidied up all the cables attached to the recording equipment. When he looked back, Michael had conjured from thin air a tray upon which stood half a dozen shot-sized glasses and a dusty, unlabelled bottle.

Phil clasped Brendan's hand warmly as he reached the group around the table. "Brendan, I've not had the opportunity tonight to thank you for offering your own personal knowledge of...community life in the area."

Brendan looked at Hugh before replying, as if giving the village elder the opportunity to speak first. Hugh returned his gaze steadily, and waited for Michael to serve a round of drinks. Taking his glass, he raised it in silent toast and paused a moment for everyone else to respond. As they settled on their seats, Father Tomàs became a model of business efficiency.

"I'll act as chairman of this meeting, if nobody minds. I think we'll need to keep the business brief."

There were no objections, and he continued. "Brendan, we've been hoping to include you in helping Phil and Kate with your invaluable knowledge and experiences, but we don't see you in town *or* in church as often as we'd like to."

There was no offense in the priest's words, and Brendan took it in the right spirit. "Sure, an' you know how it is, Father. With such a big farm, and bein' so far from the church an' all."

"Sure, an' 'tis what's in your heart that counts, no doubt," Father Tomàs replied smoothly.

Brendan nodded. "'Tis flattered I am that you'd be thinking to include me, and happy if I can make myself useful to *an Macdairmada!*"

Phil flushed. "As I've already told Father Tomàs and several others, I don't—"

"You'll excuse me, sir, for gainsaying you, but all anyone has to do is to take a look at some of the surviving portraits of the MacDermots through the years to see the likeness. I've the book itself with me, and if anyone thinks the portrait of Hugh Hyacinth doesn't resemble Phil with a different hairstyle, I'd beg to differ!"

The blue-bound volume of the Clan MacDermot family history was passed from hand to hand. Brendan had laid a bookmark at the page showing a photograph of Hugh Hyacinth, and there really could be no doubt of the family traits the two men shared. Phil felt he could easily have been looking at himself in a shaving mirror, if he could ignore the fashionable—in the seventeenth century—sculpted, lacquered, tied-back hairstyle.

Brendan looked slowly at Phil and Kate. As usual, they were side by side, holding hands.

"I know I'm speaking for us all when I say that I sincerely hope you're not having second thoughts about returning to Ardcane, or Kilronan, or even the auld Carrick on the north shore o' the lough!"

"Carrick, it's an old word for a castle," offered Hugh, seeing the blank look on Phil's face.

Brendan continued. "There's not a lot more I'd say, here and now, other than to point out that unless Phil and Kate have made a decision and are prepared to come and join us, we'd be wasting our time to make this a longer meeting."

A tense hush fell, and Phil sensed that this was a significant moment. Whatever he said or did *right now* would have enormous consequence and impact on the lives of a large number of people, many of whom were still relative strangers who hadn't even suspected his existence a few weeks previously. He stood and faced the gathering with the lightest of pressure on Kate's fingertips to rise alongside him. The look that passed between them at this juncture was also superfluous; neither had the slightest doubt.

"If you're prepared to accept us, on the basis of what you've learned of us in the past fortnight, then we're honored, and it would certainly be churlish, and a coward's way at best, if we were to decline the opportunity. For better and best, I hope, I'm honored to accept your invitation, and will do my very best to live up to the traditions expected of the clan leader, *an Macdairmada. Sláinte!*"

As one the village representatives rose and returned the toast with unfeigned pleasure mingled with perhaps a *soupcon* of relief, the glasses were drained. Then, at Michael Ashe's insistence, and following his example, they were ritualistically shattered, flung into the hearth where the turf had almost burnt out, symbol of an oath sworn that would never be broken.

Chapter Seventeen

Kate found Phil sitting at his laptop, sipping at a mug of coffee. He nodded vaguely to acknowledge her arrival.

"Kettle's just boiled. What d'you think of this?"

Kate stared. In all the years they'd known each other, she'd never known him to be less than fully alert, responsive to her presence. A few heartbeats passed, and Kate leaned forward to see what had caught his attention before the pause became overlong.

Automatically, Phil's left hand snaked upwards and outward. His fingers tangled in her hair. His right hand manipulated the mouse, scrolling through a screen completely covered with close-packed text. "I remembered a snippet of information from school history lessons," he murmured, scrolling on to a diagram and highlighting the accompanying text.

"There! Knew I'd find it. Look!" He highlighted a paragraph and enlarged the accompanying sketch. "You know where there's a small niche in the altar stone, and it usually has a small relic of some sort in it, a scrap of bone, a piece of cloth, something significant?"

Kate nodded.

"At one time, it wasn't unheard of for a sword or some other weapon to be given pride of place inside the altar stone. I found several accounts of this, dating back to the eleventh and twelfth centuries. So I've been having a closer look at this sketch, well, tracing, really. I haven't got your artistic skills. I took it from the altar stone. After all these years, it's not easy to see just whereabouts on the surface the...hole, or whatever it's called, might be. But you can just about make out a slight difference in coloring and texture, I think, and guess what? It's definitely too big for a small piece of bone or another sacred relic such as a ring, or a scrap of cloth. It's also the *shape* I was hoping it might be."

Kate stared again, totally lost, unable to follow Phil's line of reasoning.

He glanced up from the screen and gave Kate his full attention. "It's quite big compared to some I've seen in churches I've visited. Also, as I said, even the *shape* of it makes me think." He smoothed the slightly crumpled sheet of paper once again. "This is as close as I can get to the size and shape of the hidey-hole on the altar. I'll know better, I hope, when I've had a chance to take a few shots with a special camera I've asked Ray to lend me for a day or two! But the point is..." He pinned the paper flat onto a pin board and tapped it with a pencil. "I make it about twelve inches high by eighteen or so across. And since it's not likely to be too far under the surface, I reckon I'll be able to get a photograph of the object without smashing up the altar stone or damaging what's been hidden inside it." Pointing dramatically at the page with the pencil he still carried, he breathed, "I'm convinced that we'll find a certain person's *harp* concealed in the altar."

※ ※ ※

After a leisurely breakfast, Phil and Kate saw to Gerald before wandering hand-in-hand along the forest path that led to the pub. Moira was brushing in front of the door as they approached.

"There's a parcel come for you," she called, disappearing inside as she spoke.

"That was quick. It can only be the camera, but I didn't think it would get here *so* fast."

They followed Moira inside, where a securely bubble-wrapped package marked FRAGILE stood on the corner of the bar.

"I asked a friend for the loan of a special piece of equipment," he explained to Moira as he took a sharp blade and carefully peeled off the protective coverings. These he lay intact as far as possible for re-use. "We've been on Trinity Isle again," he said for Moira's benefit. "And we heard music, harp music, no question about it. If there *is* something sealed inside the altar, a couple of photographs is all I need. And if there's nothing to be found, I won't have to damage or destroy anything in the process," he concluded.

"No time like the present," offered Michael Ashe, who had arrived sometime during Phil's explanation. "Would you like myself or Hugh to accompany you?"

"The more the merrier." Phil grinned, relieved that others took his idea seriously rather than laughing outright. A further thought struck him as Sean was dispatched to invite the village's elder statesman.

"It might be a good idea, though, to send word for Father Tomàs as well. Surely this concerns him?"

A swift phone call and explanation, and Father Tomàs promised to meet them at the lake.

"We've time for a standing glass afore we leave," grunted Michael, pulling at a handpump as he spoke. "I've no doubt Hugh will look in here rather than go past, if I know him."

Hugh arrived, leaning on Sean's arm, before Michael had finished filling everyone's glass, and was included in the refreshments. Phil repeated his theories for Hugh's benefit.

"Stranger things have happened, indeed," was Hugh's comment. For some reason, Phil felt ever more certain that he had good grounds for what had at first seemed to him an unlikely scenario.

"Let's be off, then. Father Tomàs has had enough time to get here, by now," said Hugh as he drained his glass. As he placed his glass on the bar, a distant rumble made itself heard, which quickly proved to be the slightly out-of-tune engine of the parish priest's ancient Volvo. Hugh waited for a lift to save him the few hundred meters walk while the rest of the group wandered down to the lakeside.

When they arrived at the lough, Sean was already on board the skiff, ready to move off. He was clearly about to burst with pride at having the honor to act as ferryman to such an important group of local dignitaries out to Trinity Isle. "Sure, an' I can take four passengers at a time, so I can, Uncle Phil!" he cried as Phil escorted Father Tomàs the final few steps along the path to the lakeside.

"That I'm certain you can!" he replied with the most serious *mien* he could achieve. Inside, he was fair bubbling with the desire to laugh, but would not for all the world hurt the young boy's eager-to-please feelings.

"However," he continued, to cover his conflicting emotions. "In fairness to the age and stiffness of limb some of the party will have to contend with, and with due regard for any Health & Safety regulations that may have been invented since last time I looked, can I suggest you only take *two* at a time?"

After a brief inner consultation, which probably lasted at least half a second, Sean nodded gravely and allowed that this was a perfectly sensible suggestion. Upon receipt of this solemn, ratified by NATO decision, Phil quickly busied himself pairing off the waiting travelers. Kate stepped into the bow seat while Michael Ashe eased himself into the stern bench for the first crossing, and the remaining pairs were quickly transferred in their turn. Phil opted to cross with Father Tomàs on the last journey.

"You stay on the shore now, Sean," he said as the ferryman turned to cross the narrow stretch of lake one more time. "And if you go off for a few minutes, make sure there's someone to carry a message. There are no phones on Trinity Island, should we need you!" Curiously, Phil realized as he spoke that he hadn't felt the inconvenience of not having a mobile demanding his attention and/or presence elsewhere, not once throughout their brief but hectic holiday. No withdrawal symptoms either, he thought to himself, and made a mental note to speak to Kate about it when they were on their own. Perhaps it was simply the beat of a different drum, or the more relaxed view of life, but it really seemed as if things could still get done effectively *and* within an acceptable time frame without resorting to the latest technological "must have" intrusions on life.

As he turned away from seeing Sean safely on his way, Phil's heart skipped a beat. Everyone seemed to be looking at him—to show leadership, perhaps? He hesitated, and was immediately glad he hadn't done or said anything that might have made him seem foolish, or arrogant, which would probably have been worse.

They weren't waiting for his lead at all, but that of his traveling companion, Father Tomàs. The old priest slipped a stole around his neck with practiced ease and fished an ancient rosary out of a pocket of his soutane. Despite the heat of the day, he seemed to find the long black robe comfortable to wear. He glanced around the group and kissed the crucifix. Automatically, everyone made the sign of the cross.

"I'm not going to waste time saying things twice over," he said with a half-smile on his lips as he gazed directly at Phil and Kate. "But since not everyone present has the Gael, and it's too warm to repeat things, I'm restricting the prayers for guidance to the English language."

"I'm sure God understands whatever language you choose," grunted Brendan O'Hanlon who had the grace to flush when Father Tomàs gave him a curious look but said nothing.

A brief round of prayers and pleas for intercession and guidance followed before Father Tomàs indicated that Phil should explain what he hoped to do.

"Some of you might think that X-ray cameras are something that only exist in the imagination of the latest Bond film scriptwriter," he began, "but in reality, cameras that can see inside certain things have been around for some time. They're just...shall we say, *very* expensive and hard to come by, but I have a friend in the trade who owes me a professional favor, and I persuaded him to loan me one."

"And I assume *you'll* be owing *him* a favor after this," murmured Michael Ashe, provoking a round of sincere chuckles from the rest of the group, including Phil.

"I'm sure you're right about that. But that's something for me to worry about at a future date. And who knows? This story in itself might just possibly go a long way to repaying the debt if it gets media coverage."

A brief, awkward silence made Phil wonder if perhaps he ought to have considered whether or not this peaceful, isolated community would appreciate being under the microscope for the world's media if a story of such proportions were to result from their investigations. Swiftly, he wrote himself another mental note to be acted on when time presented itself.

Placing the camera on the altar, he stepped back and explained what he intended to do with it. As he moved away from the stone, Father Tomàs took his place and sketched a formal blessing in the air above it, raising a querying eyebrow at Phil before electing to sprinkle holy water from a phial in a circle around the camera where it stood rather than risk sprinkling directly onto a delicate piece of equipment.

"I'm assuming that the chapel is one of the oldest parts of the building if not *the* oldest surviving part. Is that right, Father?"

Father Tomàs nodded agreement. "That's correct, Phil. Despite three major fires that we know about, the chapel would always have been where it is now, on the easternmost wing. It's a religious tradition. Please, carry on."

Unaccountably, Phil felt more certain he knew what the camera would reveal, even from this small crumb of confirmation that he had angled for without really hoping for a positive response.

"I've learned from older records of a tradition of burying famous warriors with their favorite weapons," he continued, watching everyone's face for their reactions, relieved to see a couple of slow nods. The tradition, apparently, was not totally unknown. "What I hope this camera will reveal is a variation on the theme, so to speak." He hesitated before taking the final step. Before he could speak again, however, there was a loud gasp-cum-whistle from Brendan O'Hanlon.

"Holy Mother o' God! Beggin' y'r pardon, Father! You mean that..."

From somewhere, Phil found the confidence to complete Brendan's thought as he faltered. "Yes, Brendan! I believe the photographs I'm about to attempt will indeed show a harp buried inside the altarstone, in honor of Turlough O'Carolan's favorite 'weapon.'"

Chapter Eighteen

After such an intense and exciting preamble, the testing of the theory was almost a disappointing anticlimax.

The camera did exactly what it said on the label, and quickly revealed an unmistakeable image of a three-dimensional object of the expected roughly triangular shape, measuring some fifteen inches on its long axis, and perhaps twelve or thirteen inches across at its widest point. Two of the three sides appeared to be slightly bowed; the third, by contrast, was perfectly straight.

It only took Phil a few minutes to download a series of images from the camera to his laptop. The village committee watched in appreciative silence as he went through the process he had performed almost every day of his working life on autopilot. At length, he felt compelled to break the silence, which was starting to acquire a certain quasi-religious reverence.

"It's not rocket science, you know," he protested as he saved the final image onto his hard drive. "All I'm doing is—"

"Is something none of us have a clue about how it's done; don't belittle y'rself!" Hugh interrupted, but with such a gentle lilt to his voice it would have been impossible to take offense. Phil's shoulders had risen in involuntary defense, but he relaxed immediately and with genuine relief as soon as he realized that it wasn't going to be necessary. It was clear, everyone had decided to accept his professional skills as part and parcel of the intended *an Macdairmada*, the person they had come to know and had accepted without question into their community. Another tiny but significant step had been taken along the path he had stumbled across as if by accident but had opted to follow as a matter of conscious choice.

"Father Tomàs, I need to ask you something."

The self-appointed committee, by tacit consent, sat on the grassy lawn just outside the last remaining line of stones marking the ancient chapel's walls. Chilled Guinness bottles were being distributed and dispatched.

Father Tomàs looked at Phil, and raised his bottle silently to indicate that he should proceed.

"I'm...not exactly *au fait* with current church customs," Phil said, choosing his words carefully as he went along. "But I wonder, is there some sort of...appropriate...re-consecration ceremony or something that ought to be carried out, or at least considered, in the light of what we've established this morning?"

Father Tomàs gave the question due thought.

"I'd have to ask Bishop Delaney about that, I think," he admitted, a shade reluctantly, Phil thought. He nodded as if he had reached a solution to some inner conflict. He was clearly about to explain himself more fully when Brendan called out.

"Phil, I don't see any...markings, or discoloration of any sort on the altar! What on earth made you think there was something concealed...just where you photographed, there in the middle of the altar? Because I can't see anything at all."

With an apologetic glance to the priest, Phil unfolded his lanky frame and ambled over to Brendan. He brushed his hand over the altar's surface, caressing the warm stonework.

"I admit, some of it was guesswork, but it was an informed guesstimate, in a way," he admitted.

"For obvious reasons, and I think Father Tomàs will back me on this one, the logical place to secret a sacred object, a relic, a weapon, or even a musical instrument would be in the altar stone itself, and the most likely place will always be front and center, especially with an object that attracts a degree of reverence. Pilgrims and other visitors coming to pray, even looking for a miraculous cure, would make their pleas at the altar. That's why the altar is the natural place to conceal such objects."

"So why can't I see any signs of...plastering, or a different type of stone or something?"

"Remember what Father Tomàs told us. The altar and the chapel have *always* been in this corner of the building. So, the altar was already installed some considerable time *before* Turlough O'Carolan lived and worked here, barely four hundred years ago. And being stone, of course, it wouldn't have been significantly affected by any of the fires mentioned in the records."

Kate drifted over. There was a certain slightly puzzled look on her face, which Phil had seen from time to time. It warned him there was a question about to be asked.

"Phil, the *size* of this...this object? Roughly fifteen-by-twelve? Isn't it a bit ... *small* for a harp? Would it be possible to get a tune out of it?"

"Good point," Phil conceded as he opened a window to the Google search engine on his laptop. "I know that we all have the image of a full-size concert harp standing in the corner of a stage with nearly as many strings as a grand piano, but I've come across harps in other sizes, knee harps, and smaller lap harps, which traveling minstrels often used. In theory, at least, there's no reason why a smaller harp with these dimensions couldn't be used. I'm just grateful that I managed to get some real physical evidence without having to take a sledgehammer to the altarstone!" A thought suddenly occurred to Phil, and he turned back to Father Tomàs. "When you said you'd have to talk to your bishop about...you know..."

"About re-dedicating the chapel? I don't think there's going to be a problem, but it's a courtesy call to let him know what we're planning, and invite him to visit us if he's a mind to do so."

A swift glance passed between Hugh, Michael Ashe, and Brendan, so swiftly that Phil was for a split-second unsure as to whether he'd actually seen/sensed it or if it was a figment of his imagination. He caught Hugh's eye and refused to look away. Hugh dropped his gaze first.

"What's the problem, Hugh?"

"Bishop Delaney's a good man... Someday, he'll be a saint, I'm sure of it. But he's not a Carrick man, nor even from Roscommon, though he's been Bishop at Elphin for a number of years now. Still, he's a Kerryman, and he's never really had a sense of how we do things here in Roscommon."

"What Hugh's trying to *avoid* saying," Brendan cut in, "is

this, Bishop Tony Delaney has a tendency to talk to anyone about everything, and as soon as he finds out that something a little out of the ordinary has been going on here, he won't be able to stop himself telling the rest of the world about it."

"And we've always had a nice, quiet life in these parts," Michael Ashe concluded as Brendan paused for a moment. "So we can do without the world's media turning up!"

"Publicity! Yes, that could be a problem," Phil said with a concerned edge to his voice. Quite unbidden, unwelcome visions of attention crowded before him, destroying the tranquil pace of life in Kilronan and the other small communities around the shores of Loch Cé. He felt Kate's hand tighten over his, and knew at once that she was seeing similar disturbing scenes playing out in her mind's eye. A random thought struck him, and he wondered, how often did Kate share his other daydreams and nightmares?

"I can't really leave Bishop Tony in the dark, all the same," muttered Father Tomàs "But I think I can persuade him to keep it quiet for as long as possible, so we can finish what we're doing at the moment. It's only a question of a few more days before you two go back to Liverpool, for a while, at least."

There was a hint of a question in the delivery of this last sentence. Phil looked at Kate, then nodded and chose to answer for them both. "Give us a couple of months, three, tops, to sell what we can and bin what we can't. We'll be back here before the end of the year, assuming the house sells quickly. Last I heard, the market was getting better from the seller's viewpoint! And there's a bonus, too. We can keep the car instead of flogging it at a loss and buying a left-hand drive job if we were moving somewhere other than Ireland!"

For a few lingering seconds, a calm silence settled over the unmoving tableau on the foreshore of Trinity Isle as the full importance of this statement of final commitment sank in on each of them. Hugh O'Gara was first to stir himself, reaching out to offer Phil his hand in welcome.

"You'll allow an old man to be the first to welcome the new *an Macdairmada*, I hope! Welcome home, sir. Welcome home!"

Michael Ashe, Brendan O'Hanlon, and Father Tomàs were swift to add their sincere greetings, pumping Phil's hand enthusiastically and embracing Kate with varying degrees of bear hug.

As they concluded their exchange of greetings, a loud, melodic whistle from the shoreline was a signal that Sean had returned, ready to ferry them back to the pub for lunch.

By the time Moira had served them with a hearty, satisfying warm meal, Michael had installed himself behind the bar and began pulling pints. Phil noticed that he was filling each glass to something over the three-quarter mark and leaving it to settle, a serving technique that was normally reserved for busy sessions rather than a quiet-ish Monday midday such as this. He shrugged. If Michael Ashe had decided that there were good grounds to run off so many glasses, he must know best.

By the time they'd finished eating, the pub was starting to fill nicely. Phil realized that the "jungle drums" had been beating once more, almost inevitably due to Sean riding round the village on his bike telling all and sundry what he'd become privy to on the short drive back from the loch.

A constant stream of good wishes and congratulations were offered and accepted as the afternoon progressed, and once again, the *craic* developed into a full-blown musical extravaganza before people started drifting home to prepare their individual evening meals. Michael Ashe insisted that Phil and Kate should stand either side of him and shake hands with each departing guest, a light and far from onerous task that made Phil feel almost as if he were already the host, thanking each guest who left his house at the end of a very successful party. As the last customer left, Phil made to help with the collecting of the relatively few glasses left on the tables, but Michael Ashe would have none of it. Phil wanted to argue the point, but Moira came out of the kitchen and stopped him dead.

"Sure, an' 'tis Patsy Slattery on the phone wants to know if you can say what time she should expect you on Tuesday? The Dublin bus is due at about ten-thirty if you can make it. She can get him to wait a few minutes if you'd struggle to be there?"

The harsh realities of the world outside Kilronan, including such inconveniences as bus timetables, intruded on the casual approach to the passage of time that had become their habit during the past fortnight. Reluctantly, Phil acknowledged that this would be perfectly possible provided that breakfast could be served at about eight o'clock. With this agreed, he insisted on paying Michael Ashe the final portion of their bill before exiting the same way as everybody else and crossing the yard to feed and brush Gerald while Kate went into the caravan and packed away everything they could possibly do without.

◉ ◉ ◉

"Not so many in this evening, Michael."

Michael Ashe topped off Phil's fresh pint of Guinness with a shamrock design.

"We're not so fond of goodbyes as you might think," he replied, sliding the glass to a millimeter perfect distance from Phil's hand where it rested on the counter. Absently, Phil noted that, as usual, not the least drop spilled from the glass in the process. "Especially when we *know* someone's going to be returning soon. We'd rather say *slàn go fóill*. See you soon is probably the nearest translation."

Phil nodded. "Like the French *au revoir*, really. I guess the same way of avoiding saying goodbye probably exists in most languages," he said, taking a philosophical pull at his glass while Michael Ashe topped off Kate's drink. Languages had always fascinated Phil, and he made yet another note to himself, this time to tackle basic Gaelic in the months prior to their intended return. Perhaps there would be evening classes at Liverpool Uni—

Phil's eyes flicked to the full width of the bar mirror behind Michael as the sound of the front door opening and closing disturbed the silence. Heavy boots crossing the wooden floor announced the arrival of Brendan O'Hanlon. A tacit glance from Phil resulted in a third glass being topped off and ready by the time Brendan reached the bar.

Kate crossed the room to join them so that Phil wouldn't have to leave Brendan in order to carry her drink over.

Brendan raised his glass in silent thanks, and waited for Phil to reciprocate before drinking from it.

"I'm glad to have caught you on your own. I need a private word afore y' leave!"

"What's on your mind, Brendan? You know I'm relying on people such as yourself for advice and suggestions."

"It's just something you might not have considered, but

all the same...it's probably just as well to bear this in mind," he said.

Phil was vaguely aware of Kate's fingers closing around his as she snuggled against him.

"I think you can take it as certain that your decision to accept the title and responsibility of the *an Macdairmada* has pleased everyone in the community. But one thing you might not be aware of, and particularly as you live in England at the moment, do you know of Heraldic House in Dublin?"

Phil nodded. Heraldic House had been referred to several times in the research he'd been doing both before leaving Liverpool and again during the past fortnight.

"Particularly because the title has such a long, established history with detailed written records, you'll find that you'll have to contact them sooner rather than later to clarify a couple of practical points."

"What do I need to contact them about? Is there anything specific I should be asking?"

"There's something I think you'll need to take into account, something peculiarly Irish in nature. Have you come across something called Brehon law?"

A vague chime rang in a dusty corner of Phil's memory, but he had to shake his head after thinking about it for a few seconds.

"I've heard the term, I think, but I can't recall any of the details. How's it going to affect me...or should that be *us*?"

"Brehon law goes a *long* way back. In fact, it probably starts from days when there was an *oral* rather than a written records system," Brendan answered. "Traditionally, if you want to know anything concerning ancient laws and customs, you refer to Heraldic House for information. In fact, I think you'll find that certain Brehon laws still apply. They've never been challenged, so nobody's ever thought to repeal them!"

"Anyway, I checked a couple of websites last night, and it seems that claims to this and a couple of other vacant titles *must* go through Heraldic House. I suppose that's logical. It must prevent a lot of potential disputes, if there were ever to be more than one person claiming a title at any time."

"At least it's one thing that can just as easily be done from anywhere once I'm back in Liverpool. Yes, I *almost* said something else," he admitted with a grin. "But I have to get used to the idea that I won't be calling Liverpool 'home' for very much longer!" The amused gleam in Brendan's eye told Phil that his sense of what Brendan had been thinking was spot on. He continued. "If I understand you correctly, there aren't any other claims on the title, are there?"

"Not to my knowledge. The website was updated a few days ago at the end of August."

"Can you tell me anything else? How does this—these?—Brehon laws work?"

"A lot of them are still very much based on the oral tradition, Phil. You're going to need to check the details with the powers that be, through Heraldic House. On the other hand, it's something you can do once you're back in Liverpool. Inevitably, it's going to take time. You wouldn't have been able to do more than start making inquiries even if you'd known about it from Day One of your holiday! In many ways, I suppose you could say that they reflect the feudal nature of what society must have been like when Brehon law was effectively the only law that mattered."

Kate suddenly squeezed Phil's hand as a thought struck her. "Then that must mean that the Lord of the Manor position of the clan chief at the time must have been..."

"One of real importance, Kate. Surely you would have realized that by now?"

Phil and Kate both shook their heads. Until Brendan put it into words, neither of them had really considered this.

"Brendan, do you think these people can advise me on what my responsibilities are going to be as *an Macdairmada*? I mean, it can't be a ceremonial role, a meaningless title?"

Brendan gave this serious thought for a moment. "You know, the important thing is you've been chosen, so to speak by popular acclaim, and that's the crux of the matter. The job doesn't automatically go to the firstborn, you know. It's mostly hereditary as far as the *family* is concerned, but sometimes, the best choice for the position has been found elsewhere, a close cousin or similar."

Phil thought of the amount of family research he'd been able to carry out. When he considered it, it had in fact been pretty thorough. "I haven't come across any close relatives, and certainly none *older* than me," he said, slowly but confidently. A further thought struck him. "How about female relatives? How feudal are the rules?"

Brendan grinned.

"As far as clan leadership's concerned, that's still a male-only bastion, and I don't think it likely to change in the foreseeable future. But let's not forget that the precedent was set by Turlough O'Carolan's patron, Mary McDermott, when she survived for so many years after the death of her husband."

"Brendan, I'm much obliged for your thoughts and the information you thought to pass on about contacting Heraldic House. I'll certainly do as you suggest as soon as we're back in Liverpool, but for the moment, I think an early night for us would be a good idea. There's still Mass tomorrow morning, and what follows afterwards."

Neither Phil nor Kate were allowed to leave without shaking hands with everyone present, including a couple of familiar faces who arrived as they worked their way toward the door. Eventually, they made their escape to find Sean putting the finishing touches to a scrupulously thorough grooming of Gerald.

Kate's attention was caught by the caravan, which was half-concealed beyond the stable.

"Phil! Look at this!"

Phil had paused briefly to compliment Sean on his usual enthusiasm and eagerness to please. He looked up quickly at Kate's excited tone of voice.

Nosegays of fresh flowers had been left in small bunches all around the door and the harness rails. Many of them had notes attached that identified the donors. Some were anonymous. They were all without exception handmade and beautifully composed.

"It was mostly the girls o' the village what left them," said Sean with an expression on his face that left no room for doubt as to his opinion of the gesture.

"Well, you can tell them that *I* think it's a lovely gesture," said Kate firmly. "I won't disturb them by moving them inside, but I wish I could. I'm sure they'd make the bedroom smell lovely! I'm sure they'll still be fresh enough to boast about when we get to church in the morning." She inhaled deeply from a luxurious spray of lavender and lilacs.

Phil took the opportunity to haul Sean off to one side and tell him in no uncertain terms just how insulted he'd feel if the self-appointed groom and gofer continued to refuse to accept financial reward for everything he'd done during the fortnight. After some discussion, and not a few protests about Phil's generosity, a sum that satisfied the consciences of both parts changed hands, and they were left to pack the final few possessions before retiring for the night.

⚜ ⚜ ⚜

Gerald stood, brushed until he shone, and ready to go between the shafts when they were woken the following morning by Michael Ashe and Moira rigged out in Sunday best. The harness gleamed from yet another polishing, courtesy of Sean. A giggle of young girls, identically clothed in traditional Irish dance costume, stood in two neat lines on either side of the caravan. As soon as Phil and Kate appeared at the door, they burst into a well-rehearsed song, kept together by a flute, or possibly a whistle, played by a young lady half-hidden behind the singers whom Phil recognized as the teacher in charge of the church choir.

As they headed east out of Kilronan, every doorway had at least one adult standing, waving and smiling. The choir split into two columns and danced alongside the caravan as they trundled along the road, gradually falling behind and reforming into two close-dressed columns as they continued to dance, and the caravan was gradually allowed to pull ahead. The whole of the village seemed to be on the move. Some of the older residents had obviously set off early by whatever means of transport they could arrange. Leaving Phil to take the reins and encourage Gerald to put best foot forward, Kate trotted through to the rear of the caravan and opened the window to continue to wave to their followers until the first bend in the road hid them from sight.

"Gerald's on his Sunday best behavior, too, by the looks of it." Phil grinned as Kate rejoined him on the driving bench "Just *look* at the way he's picking up his feet!"

"Hooves," Kate corrected automatically

"Hooves? Or hoofs?" said Phil, with a childish tease in his voice

"D'you know, I'm not absolutely certain," laughed Kate. "But on the other hand, I don't suppose it matters. I doubt Gerald ever bothered to learn spelling rules!"

Phil grinned as a Disneyesque scene of Gerald and an assortment of other animals sitting at cartoon-style school desks formed itself in his mind. The class appeared to be at least nominally under the tutelage of a bespectacled owl. Even without soundtrack, Phil just knew somehow that the teacher would prove to be female, with an irritatingly fussy voice to match her attitude. Grabbing a stump of pencil and a sheet of paper, he jotted a note to himself. Perhaps it could become an amusing story when he got a moment to work on it. He paused and frowned. What on earth had made him even *think* about writing stories? He was a professional photographer, had been all his life, but there was a definite attraction about the idea of trying to write a story, especially one aimed at children.

The journey to Ardcarne was no great distance, and they shared the road with families and couples walking to Mass. Phil was concerned that Gerald might not be accustomed to large numbers of pedestrians on the road, but his fears proved groundless and they reached the neighboring village without incident or accident. Father Tomàs stood and waited at the church door with a welcoming smile on his face. The church bell began to chime, a slow, measured pulse to mark that the service would begin in fifteen minutes.

"There are benches reserved for you. I'll let you take your seats," he said, guiding them onwards with a gentle touch on Kate's elbow as he turned to greet another couple.

The church was a riot of freshly cut flowers, and the choir was already in place in front of the Lady altar. Three couples were already sitting in the reserved benches and greeted Phil and Kate with handshakes as they settled onto the pew. In the tower, the tempo of the bell increased, indicating that Mass would begin in five minutes. Father Tomàs came down the central aisle, with swift benedictions to all and sundry, and disappeared into the sacristy to don the vestments of the day.

By the time he re-entered the church through the main door, the Kilronan contingent of the choir had arrived and slotted into their places. Kate just had time to catch the first faint trace of incense overlaying the scent of the flowers before the first hymn began.

An order of service was provided on each pew; looking at it, Phil realized that it was to be a bi-lingual service, with prayers and hymns in both English and Gaelic. The opening hymn was in Gaelic, but from the first notes, he realized that it was a well-known melody that also had an English set of lyrics, though not necessarily a straight translation.

The Scripture readings were in English, which helped him to concentrate and reflect on the reason for Father Tomàs' decision to bless all marriages on this particular Sunday.

After reading the Gospel, he stepped down from the altar and came forward to stand at eye-height with his congregation rather than above them in the Lectern normally used for readings, and the thoughts and advice he would normally have given in his Homily.

"It's always grand to see so many gather here on a Sunday, and especially when I know that some of you find it difficult to make the time to worship every week. Even more pleasing is the presence of visitors to our little community from far away, and others from not so far. Now, I'll not take up a great deal o' the day with words because I wanted to make today a special day, one in which actions may prove to be far more important than words; a re-dedication of the holy sacrament of marriage."

Sitting in their center aisle reserved seats, Phil suddenly realized that they had, in effect, been elected to become the first couple to receive the intended blessing, as they could hardly give place to the next couple, sitting further away from the priest. He fingered the box containing the rings in his pocket as Father Tomàs concluded.

"So I call upon you all to witness the rededication of vows of the ten couples married this year and wish them all they might wish for themselves, in this life and the next!"

With a nod to Phil and Kate, he removed his stole from around his neck and laid it, folded, across their joined hands. Phil offered the ring box, which Father Tomàs opened, taking out the matched rings and holding them up for all to see. Incense and a sprinkling of water followed before he blessed them solemnly and placed the first one on Phil's hand and the other on Kate's. The choir began a very soft, wordless hum of a melody and continued as the other couples followed the same ritual. As the last couple returned to their seats, Father Tomàs invited any other couples who had been married for longer periods to come forward if they wished to receive the same blessing. A long double line formed instantly, and afterwards, Phil could only assume that the majority living in and around Ardcarne were married; children, and a few of the oldest present, were the only ones who did not join hands with a partner to seek the priest's blessing on their union.

There was one more small pleasant surprise awaiting them before the end of the Mass. After the final blessing, Father Tomàs paused and said, "I suppose it's the worst-kept secret in the parish, if not the Diocese, but I expect to see everyone here at the social gathering after Mass! Since the Lord has granted us such fine weather to enjoy ourselves, I think we ought to take what we have been offered and thank Him for His bounty!"

He then burst into a beautiful baritone rendering of the triumphant "*Ite, Missa Est*," which transported Phil instantly to the Liverpool parish in which he had grown up; the last place he could remember hearing the Latin text of the Mass. The answer followed exactly the same melody and Phil meant it sincerely as he joined in with the response, "*Deo Gratias.*"

By the time Phil and Kate had offered their rings for inspection and approval by everyone and his dog, or so it seemed, they were amongst the last to enter the meadow adjacent to the church grounds where a marquee had been erected in one corner. A mouth-watering aroma suggesting a range of culinary delights confirmed what was happening inside it.

Glasses were being ferried by hand over the heads of those lucky enough, or sufficiently agile, to reach the front of the drinks bar for thirsty souls standing further back. Two such glasses were deposited in Phil's hands as soon as he crossed the threshold, presumably *via* some thoughtful and observant soul who had been instructed to watch for their arrival.

The focus of attention on the food serving side of the tent was a hog of impressive proportions, which had been roasted in a barbecue pit overnight and topped off on a rotary spit during morning Mass. Before long, Phil and Kate were able to leave the refreshment area with ample portions of party food piled high on disposable plates.

Inevitably, Phil's attention was snagged by the musicians tuning up on and around a temporary stage, pallets covered with some form of rough woven fabric underfoot. His fingers itched. He was no ego-tripper, but he enjoyed singing and considered himself a fair guitarist. At the same time, he had a good idea of the standards of the local musicians he'd already heard, and wondered if he might have a chance to join in without making a fool of himself.

"*As if that's likely!*"

Phil almost dropped his plate. Kate was happily munching on a rib, but her voice was clear as a bell.

"How?"

"You shouldn't think so loud, Phil. Of *course* you're as good as—"

"But I *heard* you. I mean, *really* heard. At least, I think I did."

"Guess we *both* had one of your famous moments this time. It'll take a lot more than that to surprise me after everything that's happened to us on this holiday, Phil."

"Fair enough, and there are some things I'd *rather* keep...between ourselves anyway. I doubt others would understand."

They drifted automatically toward the temporary stage, content to share a moment's intimacy in the middle of a crowd. As they approached, two musicians engaged in what looked like an overly-complicated passage of hand gestures, which ended with one of them punching the air in triumph. The other touched his forehead and gestured to three others that they should leave the stage, and Phil guessed that he'd witnessed some form of "who-goes-first" ritual.

The group remaining on stage settled quickly in place and began a lively series of jigs and reels, flowing smoothly from one to the next and drawing a cheering, clapping crowd to the stage. After a set of half a dozen pieces, a tray of drinks appeared at one side of the stage, and the group, shiny with the exertion of their playing, gave place to the next set of performers. The itch in Phil's fingers was becoming almost impossible to live with, but he held himself in check. This wasn't his home. At least, not yet. He reminded himself that he had no automatic right to impose himself.

Something snagged the edge of his field of vision, something that felt close at hand but not actually a part of proceedings. He glanced up, focussing his gaze on the fields and roads in the immediate vicinity.

Along the road that Phil suddenly realized was the route towards Clogher and beyond, a string of four caravans was approaching, brightly painted and decorated with nosegays of fresh flowers, pulled by strong, well-groomed horses. As they reached the hedge bounding the meadow, voices raised in song, the group on stage paused mid-verse, and a child ran to open the gate, anticipating the arrival of unexpected guests. The wagons peeled off the road, keeping formation, and circled to a stop as the travelers continued their song.

> *"I'm a free-born man of the traveling people*
> *Got no fixed abode, with nomads am I numbered*
> *Country lanes and by ways were always my ways*
> *I never fancied being lumbered."*

Father Tomàs was first to reach the lead caravan, with a gracious smile on his face and welcoming arms. Phil was close behind, with Kate dancing attendance.

"Billy Lynch, you're always welcome in Ardcarne! I only wish we had the honor more often. 'Tis a pity you couldn't have been here earlier to share our Sunday service!"

Billy's eyes sought and locked onto Phil's. "The honor's mine, Father. We're not here as often as we'd like to be, but earlier this week, we were especially invited to celebrate a special occasion, and 'twould have been churlish to decline."

Phil sensed he had to make his mark, and eased forward to greet the newcomers. "Billy Lynch, it's good to see you again! Everyone here is as pleased as I am to welcome you and all your family to the gathering today. Perhaps you'll honor us with a song or two, once you've settled yourselves and had something to eat?"

Billy's eyes gleamed with pleasure as he returned Phil's greeting by clasping him around both shoulders. "As I remember, you've a rare voice yourself! We'll be glad to join in!"

By now, the caravans were parked in a neat line in a corner of the field, and the travelers themselves grouped behind their leader. Billy nodded to a young lady at his side who nodded and slipped off with the rest of Billy's extended family in her wake. Under cover of the general conversation around them, Billy dropped his voice and breathed a few words that were intended for Phil alone.

"I believe we've a few private matters to discuss, things that might be important, as you're leaving us soon. Laugh now, and if anyone asks, you can tell them I just told you a private joke."

Instinctively, Phil did as he was bid, wondering what Billy might have to say. Who was this cheerful rebel, self-styled king of a people who called no place home and no man their master? What lay behind his cryptic hints?

For the moment, it was clear that any answers would have to wait until the impromptu gathering had run its course. The musical entertainment was still gathering pace, and as one group of musicians replaced another, there was a further development. The girls from the two choirs had changed to team uniforms; Kilronan wore blue and silver, Ardcarne's choice was green and gold. They faced off in two straight lines in front of the stage, each cheered on by partisan supporters. Neither Phil nor Kate knew a great deal about the finer points of this form of competitive dancing, but that didn't prevent them appreciating the speed and complexity of their moves, the military precision of their rapid-fire steps. Even drumming on the ground rather than the sounding board of a dance floor, there could be no doubting the perfect timing of every footfall. The moves became more complex, the swirls and flourishes more and more extravagant until it seemed both teams had been transformed to whirling dervishes as they strove to outdo each other with progressively more difficult maneuvers.

In the end, it was the comparative youth of the dancers combined with the total depletion of their last reserves of stamina that decided the end of their demonstration dance. It began with the merest suggestion of a missed step, and rippled swiftly through both teams until they toppled like ninepins almost simultaneously, laughing and shrieking with delight as they collapsed onto the ground and agreed to call it a draw. The musicians who happened to be occupying the stage switched seamlessly to sing a traditional ballad full of exquisite vocal harmonies as the dancers were applauded, and in some cases, assisted, off the floor.

Phil was admiring the nimble fingerwork of one of the musicians. Suddenly, the guitarist looked up. His gaze caught Phil's and locked in place. With the merest toss of the head, he directed Phil's attention to a spare guitar on the stage. The invitation was clear, and impossible to decline. As he stepped onto the platform, Phil felt that this invitation was more like a military command, or a royal decree.

As he sat, the guitarist who had demanded his presence on stage murmured, "We'll take 'Mary of Dungloe' next. D'you know it?"

"Key of D alright?" Phil queried, and was relieved to get a confirmation nod. Three or four gentle, well-known ballads followed before the lead vocalist turned to Phil and said,

"We're all gaggin' f'r want o' lubrication. Can you handle a solo or two? Even one good, long something or other would be appreciated, but this is a case where more is better."

Phil wasn't totally unprepared for this. He'd had a repertoire list in his head even as he climbed onto the stage, half-expecting a challenge of this nature. Regardless of the casual manner in which it had been delivered, this was nothing less than a test of his mettle. He reeled off two fast and furious traditional humorous numbers, which got everyone in the right mood and clapping along. Behind him, he heard someone pick up a *bodhràn* drum and lay down a background rhythm.

As he played the final chord of the second song, a full glass arrived at his feet and he stooped to inhale half of its contents while acknowledging the applause of the crowd. As he settled himself again, the leader of the group who had called him up returned, and with a tacit nod, indicated that Phil had not quite finished singing for his supper. As he absently strummed a few chords, he caught sight of Billy Lynch standing quietly to one side, observant and attentive. There was really only one song he could sing to finish off his set...

He stood and stepped toward the microphone, which together with a pair of battered speakers, was all the technology Ardcarne could raise for an *al fresco* event.

"I'd like to offer this song in token of respect for our guests this afternoon, Billy Lynch and his family. It's an English song, but it describes a way of life that Billy and his fellow travelers have chosen."

The crowd was immediately silent, sensing perhaps that this song would prove to be far more thoughtful than the pacy, humorous verses of what had immediately preceded it.

Phil played a short introductory riff of melody line, and launched himself into the first verse.

Now the open road is calling

And my old boots are full o' holes
And I've just carved out my secret symbol
Behind a sign on the London road
I'll start from Cardiff and head for Preston
Forgotten now winter's hungry days
I'll sharpen knives or I'll edge your scissors
And polish sunshine to pay my way

In the seven verses that followed, Phil described the realities of life on the open road; the cold, the dampness and inhospitality of bad weather, the mistrust of someone—possibly more than one—in every settled community they visited, something that could, and often did, translate itself quickly into outright hostility. The song didn't have a chorus, but Phil distinctly heard people humming along by the time he reached verse three. By the time he reached the final verse, someone had added an intricate high descant countermelody, played on what Phil was fairly sure would prove to be a penny whistle. Without distracting him from the intricacies of the song he was performing, Phil wondered if this apparent ability to absorb melodies and other musical minutiae with little or no conscious effort was a peculiar trait of everyone living in the area. It certainly seemed that way.

And now the long roads are ever calling
Cold in the mornings, midday so hot
And I still easily turn my grindstone
And keep my nose red, deep in a pot
I leave from London, I'll head for Glasgow
Forgotten now winter's hungry days
I'll sharpen knives or I'll edge your scissors
I'll polish sunshine to pay my way

As the last notes died away, Phil was suddenly aware of the intensity of the silence all around the field. Even the youngest children had paused in their boisterous activities and were standing or sitting in silence, listening to every word. After a few seconds, there was a sway of movement, as if everyone had decided to take a breath at the same time, followed by a generous round of applause, cheers, and whistles. Phil laid the guitar to one side and picked up his glass to hide the blush he could feel spreading over his face.

The next group of musicians were ready to set up and start playing, and Phil escaped the stage during the few seconds of pandemonium and *melée* this invariably produced. There was no way he could avoid a sincere and warm press of compliments and handshakes, but the first chords of a new set curtailed the general press of bodies and allowed him to move away from the steps at the side of the platform.

"That was a very thoughtful song."

The words were quietly spoken, but from very close range. Phil hadn't seen Billy Lynch approach, though he'd been scanning the crowd to catch sight of him. With the least possible flicker of an eyebrow, Billy indicated they should stroll over in the direction of the four caravans, which had been pulled into a neat circle that included a large central space that gave at least the illusion of privacy from the rest of the field. Curiously, this was reinforced by a sudden drop in the volume of the music, the laughter, even the lower level buzz of chat, though Phil could clearly see that the party continued unabated.

"And the lovely Kate's right behind us."

It had been on the tip of Phil's tongue to ask, but Billy's calm, confident statement took his breath away. How could he *possibly* have guessed?

"You're an open book, Phil, and no more so than when you're thinking of Kate! It's like a radio. Someone's left it turned on, but it's drifted off station and makes a hissing noise, you know?"

Before Phil could respond, Kate stepped around the rear of one of the caravans and slid her arm around his elbow. Billy nodded, and indicated they should sit with him on a scattering of wooden crates clearly intended to be sat upon. A dozen or so were evenly spaced around a cheerful log fire. On some glowing embers at one side of the fire was a medium-sized lidded pan with wisps of steam escaping around the edges from time to time. As they sat, a girl in her late teens appeared from the nearest caravan carrying mugs. At Billy's nod, she poured into three of them, served them, and left without saying a word.

Billy lifted his to just below eye level, toasted his guests silently, and drank. Phil followed suit. Out of the corner of his eye he saw that Kate mirrored his action. The drink was hot but not scalding on the sensitive flesh of his palette. It was clear enough to make out the grain of the wood that the drinking vessel had been carved from, and tasted vaguely as if it was a form of tea, but unlike anything Phil had ever tasted before. On the rare occasions he'd accepted tea from someone rather than the coffee he would normally choose, he'd always opted for a dash of milk in the brew, but anything added to this drink would have spoiled its unique taste. He caught Billy's eye and blinked his grateful thanks, then examined the...cup? Mug? It was a curious shape, closely resembling the shape of the spade symbol in a deck of cards, and big enough to hold perhaps a half pint of liquid.

"We call them *korsa*," Billy murmured. "We've always used them, but I've no idea where they came from, or what the name might mean, if anything! It's just a traditional design I learned from my father, and so on. They're a useful measure and a convenient tool."

He leaned forward and encouraged the fire to flare by poking at the base with a solid stick. When he sat back and looked at both of them, his voice became more brisk, even businesslike.

"I'll start by saying I was pleased to hear you commit yourself to the challenge of leading the clan as *an MacDairmada*, Phil, though perhaps I should say, 'yourselves,' for to make it work it *has* to be a joint decision, and you'll need the support of an understanding wife in all your future plans. I trust you're clear on that?"

Phil discovered that at some point, his fingers had found and locked automatically with Kate's. The slight pressure from her fingertips across his as Billy spoke was all he needed to know he spoke for them both.

"There's very little we ever do separately, Billy, apart from the more...shall we say, specific of our own skills; photography for me, anything to do with art is Kate's field, as you know."

"So it was Kate who was asking about Jack Bolam and his paintings up at Knockvicar?"

This was an unexpected turn, and Phil almost fell off his crate with surprise. "Well, I suppose it was both of us, although, as far as the painting itself is concerned, it's more Kate's field. But it was a detail in the painting that we both noticed."

In a few brief sentences, Phil explained their two meetings with the animal, which until that day he had believed was pure myth, a creature that belonged unquestionably to folk legend, or stories written to entertain young children.

"And if I hadn't actually been allowed—no, *privileged*—to stretch my hand out and touch it, I might still find it difficult to believe," he ended, sounding lame and unconvincing in his own ears.

"So, this creature that seems to have galloped off the pages of a storybook, you've described it in great detail and done everything bar calling it by name."

Phil studied Billy Lynch's face for the slightest trace of scepticism, irony, sarcasm, open doubt. Billy held his gaze without blinking, and Phil felt a surge of relief as he realized that the person he felt he could turn to for an honest answer believed implicitly in what he'd witnessed.

"The only name I could ever give this vision is the one we all know, but speaking its name aloud doesn't change anything."

"It might help put things in perspective, though. Have you considered that?"

Phil hadn't. "Alright then, I'll name it for what we all know it is. Unicorn. It's a name everyone's heard, but precious few can claim to have met one."

"And I can assure you, Phil, that you're the *only* person I've met who's touched one!"

"But why *me*? And where does the creature come from? How does it fit into the bigger picture, so to speak?"

"Whoa! There's more than one question you're asking here, Phil, and even taking one at a time, we're not likely to find a full answer to any of 'em!" Billy stirred himself, drank again from his mug, and swilled the cooling dregs left in the bottom a few times before leaning forward and deliberately sprinkling them over the hottest part of the campfire.

Immediately, the tiny red and orange flames grew tall and fused together with a roar and became a pillar of blinding, shadowless silvery-white about three feet in height. A split second later, the column zipped itself from the tip downwards. The skin that peeled away coiled at the base, becoming the fringes of a mane of regal proportions around the neck of a proud head, equine in shape but adorned with a single horn in the center of its forehead. First, it looked directly at Phil, and nodded once before throwing its head back, sounding off a loud whinny. Resuming its original pose, it glanced briefly first at Kate, then at Billy, before dissolving in a flurry of sparks. A faint aroma of sweet incense hung over the fire for a few moments, masking the acrid smell of woodsmoke, and was wafted away by an errant draught of wind as the evening shades grew long.

Billy's voice came to Phil's ear in a slow, measured drawl, as if somehow thickened by the tendrils of smoke rising from the embers of the fire.

"The unicorn is mentioned in scraps and remnants of stories passed from mouth to mouth and generation to generation across Moylurg and Tara. To my knowledge, the tale has never been written down in any book. The unicorn appears from time to time in history, but cannot be called or commanded. He is always a sign of something significant afoot, and every time he has appeared, he has shown himself first to the Clan Chieftain, *an MacDairmada*. So, Phil, if anyone had any doubts—and, for the record, I *knew* as soon as we met—the fact that he showed himself to you is very important."

"Why... I mean, why now? What could be so important?"

"My guess would be to acknowledge your presence, and support your claim to the title," said Billy, calmly and with sincerity.

"Why did the painting we saw show a hunting scene? Why were they chasing after the unicorn? Not to trap or harm it, surely?" Kate asked suddenly.

Billy shook his head. "For an answer to that, you'd have to ask Jack Bolam himself, but since you're leaving soon, I'll remember to ask him on your behalf next time I see him."

"Oh, you do know him, then? I was wondering about that."

"Jack's another footloose, wandering soul. He and I have a lot more in common than many people think. He 'sees' things, and captures them on canvas in a way I could never hope to copy."

Kate nodded. She knew exactly what Billy was trying to say. "But Jack couldn't possibly have been painting something he'd actually *seen*," she persisted, "because it's obviously a historical setting of some sort. I remember thinking that at the time! The clothing of the riders, their weapons..."

"I can tell you this much," Billy interrupted, "because

Jack told me when he presented the painting to the restaurant. He said he woke from a dream, a really vivid dream, and felt he *had* to sketch it out immediately before he forgot the details. He said the unicorn had whispered of a great sickness sweeping the county, coming in from the West. It was a clear warning to retreat indoors. I believe it was a reflection, or an echo, from the time when the plague was rife, possibly the very epidemic that robbed Turlough O'Carolan of his sight as a young man."

"You mean they aren't *chasing* the unicorn; they're actually *following* it to safety!" Phil burst in. Once he'd put it in words, it seemed a simple, logical answer to the puzzle.

Billy nodded once more. "For what it's worth, that's my opinion. But the thing to remember is, the unicorn has chosen to show himself to *you*, Phil. Kate and I have been privileged to be in your presence, and that's the only reason we've also caught sight of him. Like it or not, Phil, the unicorn has simply confirmed his approval of you as candidate.

The miles seemed to flow by seamlessly. The early morning was neither too warm nor too chill, and with warm drinks provided by Kate, after several heavy hints from Phil, it seemed as if Patsy Slattery's livery yard appeared out of nowhere long before they were mentally prepared to end the most eventful fortnight of their lives. There could be no doubt about it; Gerald was indeed pulling hard, straining every muscle in his eagerness to return to his own stable.

Patsy was waiting in the courtyard as they fairly rattled up the packed-dirt twin rutted lane that led from the B road and onto the farm. It crossed Phil's mind fleetingly to wonder how she could have known to anticipate their arrival so closely, but then he assumed that she had heard them trundling up the track. They certainly hadn't been trying to conceal their arrival, after all.

"Sure and welcome back, the pair of youse! Have you had a good time then? And did that rascal Michael Ashe look after youse properly? I meant what I said about putting a hex on his beer if he didn't, you know."

The non-stop, breathless questions continued as she unhitched Gerald and threw a blanket over his back before leading him into the stables and starting to rub him down. The steam from his recent exertions rose, a palpable miasma shimmering in the air. A young girl entered from the far end of the stable, carrying a stainless steel bucket of something that even to Phil smelled as if it was something a horse would find irresistible.

"Patricia will carry on with Gerald. You've almost an hour before the bus is due, and I've made some tay."

This time, and with at least one eye on the clock, most of the time, there was no opportunity for the grand scale "tay" they'd been served by Patsy on arrival, but there was more than enough to keep them happy and Phil was pleasantly surprised to discover that traveling a relatively short distance in a caravan was excuse enough to work up an appetite, even though it hadn't been a physically demanding journey.

"Let me take our luggage and put it in the back of the Land Rover," Phil said as he drained his cup and glanced at the clock on the dining room wall.

"And I can help you take out the dishes," Kate insisted in a manner Phil had come to recognize as her "take no prisoners" voice. Without giving Patsy a chance to protest, she stood and began collecting crockery.

Phil asked Patsy for the car keys, and headed for the courtyard to complete his task.

◉ ◉ ◉

Kate placed the first lot of plates and saucers in the sink and turned swiftly to collect more, brushing lightly against Patsy as she turned. Patsy stiffened and laid a hand on Kate's upper arm. "Have you told Phil yet?"

Kate wrinkled her nose and looked blankly at Patsy. "Told him...what?"

With the lightest suggestion of pressure, Patsy turned Kate sideways and placed her free hand across Kate's stomach.

Although it was far too early to be anything other than wild coincidence, Kate felt what she could only describe as a curious shift in the pit of her stomach.

Kate looked intently into Patsy's deep green eyes. "You mean?"

Patsy nodded. "And there's no danger in telling either. The boyo will be a perfect child in every possible way, Kate. In fact, considering how long you've both been trying, I think you should tell Phil as soon as possible."

Patsy saw them safely on board the bus, which was perhaps half-filled with a cross-section of humanity with diverse reasons for traveling toward Dublin that day. The general hubbub and chatter didn't seem appropriate, somehow, for the news Kate had to impart. It was a couple of hours later, in a secluded corner of Dublin Airport, when she had her first opportunity to pass on her news.

Somewhat to Kate's surprise, the normally skeptical, practical Phil had no hesitation in accepting Patsy Slattery's unsubstantiated prophesy regarding Kate's revelation.

"I don't *feel* any different. I can't possibly *look* any different! And while I'm sure she's right, I'm still amazed you, of all people, are prepared to accept it without."

"Some proof? Kate, sweetheart, after all the other things we've seen, heard, and lived through this past fortnight, why should I be surprised to learn something far more natural has occurred during the same period? It's as if everything else we could possibly have wanted, even without knowing that we actually *wanted* them, has happened just as we would have wished during this holiday. Why should one more thing be any great surprise? You know we've both wanted this for...oh, I don't know."

"For 'yonks,' maybe?" teased Kate, reminding Phil of the somewhat *passé* slang term that had fallen from his lips when they were planning the trip.

Phil snorted with amusement, narrowly avoiding inhaling his Jameson rather than sipping at it. Before he could think of a fitting riposte, their flight was called and they made their way toward the check-in gate.

Sitting at a window seat as the plane eased its way up toward the thin cloud layers and the designated flight path for the short hop to John Lennon Airport, Kate turned her head to look back at the green and pleasant land they were leaving behind, if only for a short while. She stared backwards until they entered the clouds and the last vestigial traces of Ireland disappeared. Sighing, she relaxed into Phil's arms. She'd always thought of herself as pretty much of a home bird and felt most comfortable in the town in which she'd been born and lived all her life. Now, suddenly, it seemed a large, clumsy, dirty, and most unwelcoming prospect to be returning to. For no real reason, she shuddered.

Phil felt it and looked at her gravely. "Catching a cold, love?"

"No, not that. I just felt a bit...so-so about going back to Liverpool, even for such a short while. And, get this! Remember, it's your *wife,* Kate, saying this! But I don't think I can ever think of Liverpool as home ever again. Does that make sense? Can you even believe you've just heard me—*me!*—saying it?"

"Yes, sweetheart, I do. And that's a fact." Phil gently placed his free hand behind Kate's neck and pulled her slowly toward him to place a long, lingering kiss upon her lips, scandalizing a number of elderly ladies returning from pilgrimage to Knock.

At exactly that moment, had they but known, the same action was mirrored between the shades of Tomàs Laidìr Costello and Una Bhàn for a non-judgemental audience of two squirrels on the grassy knoll before the ruined Chapel of Her Dreams on Trinity Island.

About the Author

Born in the Year of the Tiger, Paul's natural curiosity combined with the deep-seated feline need to roam has meant that over the years he's never been able to call any one place home. His wanderlust has led him from one town to another, and even from one country to another.

He has always followed his instincts without question or complaint, and in true cat fashion it seems he has always landed on his feet.

"I can't remember a time when I didn't write – my father claims to possess a story I wrote when I was six, which filled 4 standard school exercise books! What I do remember from that time was being told off for doing the Liverpool Echo crossword before he got home from work! Perhaps it was the catalyst of breathing the same air as Hans Christian Andersen. While I was living in Denmark, I allowed myself to be persuaded to write for a purpose instead of purely for my own amusement."

Paul has had a short play selected for a performance at the Edinburgh Fringe Festival and hopes to one day buy a plot of land (Castle Island on Lough Key, County Roscommon) and rebuild the castle on said island, which used to belong to my ancestors.

Yes, the location of "The Chapel of Her Dreams" is a real place!

Lightning Source UK Ltd.
Milton Keynes UK
UKHW012004101219
355113UK00003B/135/P